The Pirate Queen and the Half-Plucked Chicken

To Mikey.

Enjoy the book!

Christer Sh___

The Pirate Queen and the Half-Plucked Chicken

Christopher Stevens

This paperback edition first published in 2023
by Paradice Publishing

Copyright © Christopher Stevens 2023
Cover illustration by Maria Ward

British Library Cataloguing in Publication Data
Stevens, Christopher
Title: The Pirate Queen and the Half-Plucked
Chicken
Type: Fiction. Novel
1st Edition 2023

ISBN 978 1 7393281 0 8

With special thanks to my wife, Emma, who has managed to put up with both me and my ideas for more than 38 years. Also to my children, Charlie and Tom, who provided the inspiration for this story.

My thanks too to my great friend Rod Heikell, for his guidance, encouragement and introduction to the world of self-doubt! Last but not least to his wife Lu, for her invaluable feedback and hours of patience.

Table of Contents

Chapter 1:   An Unexpected Discovery

The children ran into the kitchen, slamming the backdoor behind them.

'Just in time,' said their mother as the heavens opened.

'We saw it blowing in across the bay and ran. Lizzie didn't have a coat on.'

Mrs Baldwin turned and continued clearing the shelves.

Above the hammering of the rain, the hum of an engine was getting louder. Then it stopped. Visitors.

Charlie and Lizzie ran into the hallway as the doorbell rang and stopped dead in their tracks. There stood two of the most frightening men they had ever seen.

Mr Baldwin rose from his chair in front of the fire, walking past the children who stood there transfixed. He was lucky to stay on his feet as he clicked the latch and the wind blew the door wide open. The sudden gust and accompanying bullet-like rain brought Charlie and Lizzie back to their senses.

Almost identical, Edward and Peregrine Wolfe stood there, stone-faced. Tall, thin men, they would have been even taller had they not had a stoop. With their near black eyes, hooked noses, thin lips and rather long, greasy hair, they would have been just as at home in a chamber of horrors as they were in the real world.

'Wolfe and Wolfe. We're here for the furniture.'

Charlie stared. Who were these vultures? Granny had only gone to hospital three months ago, and it was now just two weeks since the funeral. So many people they'd never even heard of were circling around.

Granny's house was glorious. It lay within the walled grounds of a castle, which meant going through enormous gates every time you wanted to visit. Being an adventurer, the entire place was full of souvenirs she had collected on her travels. There were so many exciting things. But it was already changing. The arrowheads and spears from Africa, blowpipes and poisoned darts from South America, once proudly displayed on the wall, sat boxed in the corner and ready to go. The one thing they weren't getting their hands on was Granny's old, sweat-stained pith helmet. It was something that had accompanied her on every expedition and now lay hidden in the children's wardrobe for safekeeping.

Anything that was unwanted or simply too big was being taken off for auction. And this is where the Wolfe brothers came in. They were the best, or more precisely, the only auctioneers in the region.

'Right Charlie,' said Mr Baldwin, 'if you and Lizzie want to make yourselves useful, you can clear out the drawer at the end of the kitchen table.'

The drawer in question was a very special drawer, for it was the one that their grandfather, Toe, had kept no end of things in. No matter what you needed, it paid to check here first. Toe was an academic, adventurer and inventor who had died some 5 years ago now, but some things, including his drawer, remained exactly as he had left them.

Charlie looked at his sister and hesitated. Ever since he lost both grandfathers in the same year, change had terrified him. He'd even hated the move to High School last year. The funny thing was that everyone remarked on how tough he was just because he had a scar in the corner of his eye. You don't have to be tough to be hit by your sister's boomerang from point blank range. With her mop of brown hair and big brown eyes, Lizzie was told that she looked "exactly" like her elder brother, something she didn't appreciate at all. To her mind, she was prettier, skinnier and far more sporty, even though she'd been wearing glasses for the last two years.

'Come on children, we haven't got all day.'

Charlie trudged over to the sink and grabbed a couple of bin bags as the memories came flooding back. This had been the table where for as long as they could remember they had sat around, eating and playing whilst Granny had prepared food and recounted tales of her many exploits. The table was supposedly three hundred years old and bore the marks of time. Charlie ran his finger along a deep gouge. Something sharp had made this; an axe, a sword perhaps.

The drawer was positively cavernous, being almost as wide as the table and extremely long. The children pulled it out inch by inch, doing so with increasing care as they neared the end so it didn't drop on their toes. They plucked out goodness knows how many types of tape, screwdrivers, pen knives, old plugs, fuses, playing cards, and batteries. And loads of old tobacco tins containing everything from fishing flies to old pennies. Progress slowed down considerably as Lizzie started going through the coins one by one.

'Look Charlie, this one's got Queen Victoria on it. 1899.'

'Come on Lizzie, let's just get it over and done with.'

With a loud snap, she shut the tin.

'All done?' said Charlie.

'Hold on, I can see one last screw at the back. It looks like it's caught in the edge.'

Lizzie reached in and with one big yank pulled the screw clear, bringing with it the bottom of the drawer. And there lay a map. They looked at each other, speechless.

'It was a false bottom,' said Charlie, his eyes out on stalks.

'It looks extremely old. Do you think Granny knew about it?'

'I doubt it. I don't think it would be here if she had. Hmm, it's not finished.'

'You think someone surprised whoever was drawing it?'

'It makes sense. Surprised at best, and at worst,' Charlie looked at Lizzie stone-faced and ran his index finger across his throat from left to right.

The map looked brittle and yellowed with age and showed little detail. The only thing interrupting the outline of the island were two words, "Gravedigger's

Bay". And in the top right-hand corner there was a black flag depicting a smiling skull on top of a pair of crossed cutlasses.

Heavy footsteps echoed in through the kitchen door, and Lizzie slipped the false bottom back in the drawer covering the map. Not a second later, the Wolfe brothers shuffled in, accompanied by the pungent smell of mothballs.

'You finished?'

'Yes sir,' said Charlie, trying to sound as calm as possible.

The Wolfes took one end of the table each and started towards the front door. Although the doorways were enormous, so was the table, and the children couldn't help smirking slightly as Peregrine Wolfe (well, that was just a guess because it was equally likely to have been Edward) caught his finger between the table-top and the door frame.

'Bloomin, blasted,' he muttered.

With the Wolfe brothers concentrating on their job, Charlie tugged Lizzie deeper into the kitchen, out of earshot.

'Why didn't you grab it?'

'Sorry, I panicked.'

'Well, we need to get it back, and fast.'

The light was fading outside, giving Lizzie an idea. 'Where's Glen?' she yelled, winking at her brother.

Glen, the Baldwin family's border collie, hated storms. In fact, he could normally sense them coming. As soon as he did, he would find the smallest place to curl up and hide, often resulting in rather lengthy searches.

'I don't think I've seen him in the house. Grab your coat, Lizzie, we'd better check in the outbuildings.'

Seconds later, the backdoor slammed shut, as the children, torches in hand, ventured out into the storm. They waited in silence in one of the outbuilding doorways until the Wolfe brothers had loaded the table into the van and headed back inside the house.

'Come on,' said Charlie, running out into the pouring rain, 'it's now or never.'

The Wolfes had pulled the back of the van down to keep things dry, so Charlie reached down and, with one big heave, pulled it with all his might. It moved up about halfway with little resistance, then stopped. Lizzie turned on her torch and shone it in. There was the table, so close they could almost touch it.

'I'm hopping in,' said Charlie, putting both hands on the cold, wet metal.

He was about to jump when, above all the noise of the wind and the rain, they heard a low and steady rumble to the right of the table. Lizzie directed her torch towards the sound. There, to meet it, were two dark brown eyes and an array of white, forbidding teeth. As the growling became more pronounced, the dog rose, and drool dripped ominously from its mouth. Charlie and Lizzie, eyes still firmly fixed on the dog, slowly retraced their footsteps back towards the outbuildings and the safety of the house. The dog stood in the back of the van on guard, watching as the children made one last lunge towards the backdoor and safety.

'Did you find Glen?' asked Mr Baldwin.

'No,' said Lizzie, 'he must be inside somewhere. We'll have another look.'

They took off their coats and wellies and started the laborious and, to their minds, unnecessary search of the house. But it gave them time to think. Now and then they lifted something to check underneath or kicked a piece of furniture, but their minds were elsewhere. Eventually, they found the poor chap, curled up in a quivering heap under the bed in the guest bedroom. The time it had taken to find him had seemed like hours to the children, who had been busily whispering to each other about what on earth to do next. One decision they had entirely agreed upon was not to risk being savaged by the rather scary looking dog in the back of the van.

'Did you find him?' said Mr Baldwin as the children came back down the stairs.

'Yes,' said Charlie, 'he's under the bed in the spare room. Dad, Lizzie and I have been thinking, why don't we keep the table? It would look great in our kitchen at home.'

'I've already tried to persuade your mother, but she's right, it's just too big for our kitchen and we already have Auntie Eileen's table in the dining room.'

Charlie and Lizzie nearly jumped out of their skins as a voice boomed out, only inches behind them.

'Did either of you children see anyone outside a minute ago when you were looking for your dog? Someone's been near the van, left the back half open. They were lucky too; Lucifer could have had their arm off.'

'We didn't see anybody,' said Lizzie, trying to control the quiver in her voice as the words "could have had their arm off" resonated in her ears. 'Who's Lucifer?'

'He's the Doberman, a real softy. As long as he knows you, that is.'

'Could you introduce us?' asked Charlie in a flash. 'Lizzie and I love dogs.'

'Not today, filthy weather out there, perhaps another day,' said Edward, or was it Peregrine, Wolfe? 'Anyway, only a few more bits to sort out and then we'll be on our way.'

There really wasn't much more Charlie and Lizzie could do for the time being, other than try to think up their next plan. What could they do when the map was in the drawer, the drawer was in the table, and the table was in the van, with a dog that would happily tear you limb from limb!

Half an hour later, Mr Baldwin was at the front door with the Wolfes.

'So, it's just the large oak wardrobe and the chest of drawers, we'll be back for those tomorrow if that's ok? Sorry about that, thought we'd be able to fit it all in, we should've bought the bigger van.'

'No problem at all, any idea what time?'

'Same time tomorrow afternoon ok, about 3 o'clock?'

'That'll be fine. See you then.'

'See you tomorrow.'

There was the usual shaking of hands and the brothers sloped off into the rain towards the van. As they got in, they didn't notice the two pairs of eyes watching them like hawks from the landing window. And as the engine sparked into action and the headlights went on, Charlie and Lizzie looked at each other in desperation as the map drifted away in the darkness until it disappeared from sight. Hopefully not for good.

Chapter 2:   Now to Plan B

'We need to get that map back, Lizzie.'

'How are we going to do that?'

'I'll think of something. Haven't you seen what's been happening? They're selling all of Granny's stuff. Soon everything will be gone. This isn't any old map,' Charlie said, increasing desperation in his voice.

'It's GRANNY's map,' said Lizzie, anticipating her brother's next sentence.

'Precisely. Anyway, they're coming back tomorrow afternoon. That gives us plenty of time to come up with something.'

A day seems like a long time, unless that is all the time you have. As the evening wore on, so the ticking of the grandfather clock got louder and louder.

'Time for bed,' said Mrs Baldwin, walking into the living room. 'That's enough television for tonight.'

'Can't we stay up a little longer?' pleaded Charlie. 'It is the holidays.'

With all that had been going on, Mrs Baldwin wasn't in a holiday mood, and although she could still draw on her apparently inexhaustible supply of stamina, there was nothing she appreciated more than a little "me time" in the evening.

'Sorry children, but it's gone 9 o'clock and we have loads to do tomorrow.'

'But we still have to…'

'No, Lizzie,' growled Charlie. It was a toss-up who he was angrier with, his mother for making them go to bed so early or Lizzie for almost spilling the beans.

Up in their room, the discussions continued, but the day's exertions had taken their toll and it wasn't long before all fell silent.

The children awoke to the sound of Glen barking at the front door. It was getting light outside, and he had decided that it was time for a little wander. They grabbed their dressing gowns from the back of the bedroom door and traipsed off downstairs.

'So, what's the plan? You're the brainbox.'

Charlie was clever, but he hated being reminded of it. To his mind, it brought too much expectation, and anyway, there was always someone more intelligent out there.

'I think we just have to tell Mum and Dad the entire story. They'll definitely get the table back after that.'

'I agree,' said Lizzie without hesitation.

The children put the kettle on and five minutes later, were in their parents' bedroom with two nice hot cups of tea.

'Alright,' said Mr Baldwin, 'what do you want?'

'We found a treasure map in the kitchen drawer,' blurted out Lizzie, unable to contain herself.

'Let's see it then. It sounds very exciting.'

'It's still in the drawer,' said Charlie.

'And you want me to get the table back from the Wolfes, I suppose?'

'Well, yes.'

'I admire your ingenuity, but the answer's still no.'

11

'But it's true Dad,' said Lizzie. 'Mum, make Dad listen, please.'

Mrs Baldwin was in a different world. She was staring blankly at the wedding photograph of her parents on the windowsill.

'MUM.'

She shook her head to regain her senses and looked at Lizzie wide-eyed.

'I agree with your father,' she said, not having a clue what they were talking about.

'I'll tell you what, children. I'll call the Wolfes and get them to bring the map over this afternoon.'

'You can't do that. They'll see it,' said Charlie in utter amazement.

'Let's hear no more about it then,' said Mr Baldwin, pleased at how easy it was to call their bluff. 'Now, let's get our skates on. We've got a lot to do today.'

Charlie and Lizzie left the room in silence, heads bowed.

Mr Baldwin looked across at his wife and remembered when they first met as children. Their fathers were working on a project together, and he'd only gone along for the ride. She was with her father in his workshop and was quite different from any girl he'd ever met. Her face was dirty, as were her dungarees, and she was busy making something on a lathe. She'd looked up at him with her big green eyes, and as she smiled, he noticed her front teeth that crossed ever so slightly. Her black hair was scruffy and very short, giving her a tomboy look. Later that day, she told him she cut it herself, so it didn't get in the way. As for him, she said that she spotted something the first time she looked into his thoughtful blue eyes. Best of all, he let her get on with things, which suited her down to the ground.

Halfway across the landing, Lizzie stopped and faced her brother. 'He didn't believe us,' she said in disbelief.

'That's because we've both told the odd fib or two in the past. Remember the vase?'

'That was an accident,' said Lizzie, now bolt upright, looking Charlie straight in the eyes.

'Quiet now, Lizzie, I need to think.'

After breakfast, Charlie got the Ordnance Survey map down from the bookshelves and retired to his bedroom. Wolfe Manor wasn't far. If he took the cross-country route, he'd be there in 45 minutes. The excuse was easy, walking Glen, which had the added advantage of keeping their parents happy.

Lizzie walked in. 'Got anywhere yet?'

'I'm going to look for it while the Wolfes are here. They must have somewhere they store everything, an old barn or something like that.'

'Well, I'm coming too.'

'It'll mean going through Haunted Wood. Wooooooo.'

'Stop it, Charlie. You'd believe in ghosts too, if you'd seen what I'd seen. Anyway, I'm coming like it or not, or I'm telling Mum and Dad.'

'That's the most stupid thing I've ever heard. Talk about shooting yourself in the foot.' He hesitated. 'Ok,

I'll let you come, but promise you'll do everything I tell you to.'

'I promise.'

'OK, we leave at 2 o'clock.'

They didn't need to take much, remembering what Toe had told them when they were young. "You can solve 90% of problems if you carry three things in your pockets at all times, a penknife (preferably Swiss Army with all the gadgets), a piece of string and a small pocket torch." It had worked for him, so it should work for them.

With the preparation done and Charlie's alarm set to go off at 2pm, they ventured outside. What a day it was after yesterday's storm, a crystal clear sky, threaded by brilliant white vapour trails. In the distance, Puffin Island rose from the sea like a giant green turtle, and behind them lay the mighty Snowdon, rising majestically with a dusting of windswept snow.

They played with Glen to pass the time, and it didn't seem long before their mother was calling them in for lunch.

Charlie needn't have set his alarm. They sat there, hollow feelings in their stomachs, watching the clock tick second by second. At the stroke of two, they jumped to their feet.

'Thanks for lunch Mum, we're going to take Glen for a walk on the beach, so we might be a couple of hours,' said Charlie.

'You haven't eaten much. Are you both OK? Remember to take care. It's very shallow, so the tide comes in faster than you think.'

Charlie and Lizzie put on their coats and wellies, checked their pockets for the essentials, grabbed the lead and shouted 'walkies' to Glen. In less than two seconds, he was at the door, barking and ready to go.

They allowed themselves plenty of time to get to Wolfe Manor and sauntered through the woods towards the sea. They came to an enormous field full of cows, who took quite an interest in the invading party. As the cows approached, Charlie and Lizzie's walk turned into a jog, then a fully fledged run. But the faster they moved, so did the cows, and they were gaining on them all the time.

'Come on, hurry!' said Charlie in a mild panic as Lizzie finally got to the fence, clambering over just in the nick of time.

Hearts pounding, they climbed down the bank to the beach. With any luck, that was the excitement over for the afternoon. They kept Glen occupied by throwing an old bit of driftwood, but they made excellent progress and arrived at the pine woodland with time to spare.

With every step closer to the woods, Lizzie's heart raced faster, her mind flashing back to that fateful night when she saw the figure at the end of her bed, motionless, watching.

'Lizzie, come on, you're daydreaming.'

Think of the map, Lizzie, think of the map, she kept repeating to herself.

Haunted Wood had an unnatural feel to it. The smell of rotting wood and fungus filled the air, with the interlocking branches forming a near impenetrable blanket, keeping it in its state of nocturnal decay. Local legend had it that on windy nights, you could hear the moans of the 65 quarrymen, buried alive in the great disaster of 1798, now making their way home.

As the last remnants of daylight disappeared behind them, a small glimmer appeared in the distance and the children gave enormous sighs of relief. From now on, caution was paramount. Charlie and Lizzie kept their eyes peeled for signs of movement and listened for abnormal sounds, although the covering of pine needles meant that the entire wood was eerily silent. A small gust arrived, and the trees danced, branches rubbing together, creating a gentle moaning sound. A shiver shot down Lizzie's spine and she reached out for Charlie's hand. Was the sound really coming from the trees? Perhaps the wood was haunted? All fell silent, and with Glen pulling them along, they crept forward. Then, from only a few feet to their left, there was the crack of a branch underfoot. They stopped in their tracks, gently turning their heads towards the sound, wide-eyed, hearts beating like drums. Something was there behind the tree, and for some unknown reason, maybe Glen giving them a false sense of security, they eased towards it.

They moved their heads to one side to see round the tree, and almost jumped out of their skins as a fallow deer, as surprised to see them as they were to see it, bolted into the distance. They took a few deep breaths and continued on.

As they neared the edge of the wood, they saw the outline of Wolfe Manor. Like its owners, it was from a bygone era, with its slate-grey, castellated walls, complete with towers on each corner.

Charlie and Lizzie, keeping well hidden, spotted the Wolfes' van on the drive. Minutes later, the sound of voices cut through the silence as the brothers rounded the corner, jumping into the van and driving off.

Once they were safely out of sight, Charlie looked at Lizzie. 'Come on, we should have about half an hour to find the map and get the heck out of here.'

They sprinted across the lawn to the front of the house. Ahead of them stood a recently renovated stable block. There were several stable doors, each with a window beside it, and two larger carriage doors at the end.

'That's what we're looking for, Lizzie. Let's go.'

Once there, Charlie gave his sister a leg up so she could scan the room through the central window.

'Can you see anything?'

'We're definitely in the right place. It's jam-packed with all kinds of furniture. Best of all, it's one massive room, so if we can get in somewhere, we'll be able to check the lot.'

Unsurprisingly, the doors were all securely padlocked, but as they edged along looking for a way in, Charlie spotted something.

'Look, this padlock hasn't been closed properly,' he said, twisting it around and easing the door open.

17

Lizzie was right; the interior walls were gone, leaving one enormously long room. From that perspective, things were grand. Annoyingly, the Wolfes had covered absolutely everything with dust blankets. Finding the table was going to take longer than they thought.

'Let's split up. You check over there and I'll check over here.'

As they raced up and down the rows of furniture, lifting blankets as they went, Charlie noticed a large wet patch on the floor by one of the carriage doors.

'I reckon this is the door they used.'

Knowing that time wasn't on their side, they set about looking under the blankets closest to the door as quickly as humanly possible.

'Here it is!' said Lizzie not a minute later, as she threw back a blanket to reveal the table.

They had agreed beforehand who would do what, so as Charlie kept a lookout, Lizzie busied herself with retrieving the map. It was tricky though, with so little room to manoeuvre, but she eventually got the drawer open.

'Who's there?' came a man's voice from the other side of the open door.

Quick as a flash, Charlie and Lizzie, with Glen in tow, dived under the table, pulling the blanket back down behind them.

The door swung open, clattering against the outside of the building as the man walked in. The thudding footsteps that entered were those of a big man. If he had meant his entrance to be intimidating, he had done the trick.

'I know you're in here. You left the door wide open.'

The children stayed motionless as the man slowly and methodically edged closer, checking under each dust blanket as he went. Charlie and Lizzie looked at each other without uttering a word. Thankfully, Glen wasn't making a sound, in part because Charlie was holding his mouth closed, but he instinctively knew that something was wrong.

The man was so close the children could make out his laboured breaths, their nostrils filling with the odour of stale sweat and cigarettes. He stopped directly in front of the table, his boots in plain sight. Lizzie gulped. The drawer, it was still open, and it had stopped the blanket halfway down.

'Gotcha!' he roared triumphantly, pulling the blanket clean off the table.

Chapter 3:   So Who Knows What?

The colossus gazed down, his blood boiling.

Moments before, Charlie, having seen the events unfolding, grabbed Lizzie and Glen and rolled beneath the adjacent table. The man, sensing his prey was close, searched with increased urgency, Charlie and Lizzie somehow staying one step ahead, scrambling silently from table to table. Glen, enjoying the excitement, let out a single, high-pitched bark. In a heightened state of rage, the man started throwing not only the blankets to one side, but the tables and chairs too. He was like a bull in a china shop and getting nearer. Charlie tapped Lizzie on the shoulder and pointed towards the door. They scurried under cover to within touching distance. From here, they would be in open view. They only needed one chance, and finally the bull took a wrong turn. Charlie lifted the blanket and peered out. The man was by one of the carriage doors. Eventually, he turned away, and the children sprinted for the door.

Outside, they ran for their lives, only looking back once they had reached the safety of the woods. They lay there motionless, waiting, watching, until the hulk of a man exited. He clicked the padlock shut and peered around the garden before walking off towards a wheelbarrow.

'He must be their gardener,' said Charlie. 'It wouldn't surprise me if he's learnt his skills in prison.'

'I'm not worried about the gardener. What about the map? Have we got a Plan C?'

Charlie shrugged his shoulders.

Not wanting to hang around any longer than necessary, the children raced home. Now that they knew what being terrified genuinely felt like, any concerns about Haunted Wood or marauding cows were put firmly in their place. As they turned the last corner and the house came into view, they saw the Wolfe brothers' van pulling away.

For the next few days, the children, although despondent, never stopped trying to come up with another plan to get their hands back on the map. One thing was for sure though, everything would be under lock and key at Wolfe Manor from now on, so any foray in that direction would be fraught with danger.

Mr and Mrs Baldwin, knowing nothing of what had occurred, kept on with their daily routines of packing and tidying. Granny had rented her house for over 50 years, so although it meant that there wasn't the worry of trying to sell the place, there was the pressure of vacating it and leaving it in perfect order, as she would have wanted. But the task was a long one, with constant stops to gaze at photographs or reminisce about happier times and the clothes worn or an object bought. Mrs Baldwin was often in a world of her own, holding back the tears, subconsciously touching her mother's engagement ring or Granny Bonner's locket, both passed down the generations and which she now wore. Mr Baldwin stayed strong, which he had to for the sake of his wife. As for Charlie and Lizzie, they understood enough to keep their heads low and stay out of trouble.

Almost a week had passed since the children's visit to Wolfe Manor, and they were both becoming resigned to never seeing the map again. Then, when they had all but given up hope, they finally had some luck. It happened on a shopping trip into town, an advertisement catching their eye. Tomorrow at 2pm, the Wolfe and Wolfe furniture auction. Charlie and Lizzie got to thinking. If the table was in the auction, it would be there for people to see. If it was there for people to see, then it was there for people to touch. Hmm, there could be an opportunity here.

'Hey, Dad,' said Charlie, 'the auction's tomorrow. Wouldn't it be fun to see how Granny's things do? I'm sure there will be loads of other stuff there too, and we've never been to an auction before. Please can we go, PLEASE?'

It was rather cunning of Charlie. He knew his father had an eye for a bargain and, for some time now, had been looking for a nice, comfortable armchair. He was always complaining that there wasn't anywhere he could relax in front of the fire and read a book in peace.

'Perhaps they'll have a few armchairs too.'

Bullseye. He looked up instantly.

'Yes, let's have an afternoon off and see how Granny's things get on.'

'It'll be worth getting there early too Dad, we wouldn't want to miss anything. How exciting, my first auction. I wonder if they'll have anything I can afford. I might take my Christmas money just in case,' Lizzie said, thinking out loud.

The plan had worked, the first part of the plan, anyway. Now they had to check that the table was in the auction. Their father had already explained to them on the way home that sometimes things needed repairing, so it wasn't certain that they would see all of Granny's items go under the hammer.

As soon as they got through the door, the children asked their mother if they could borrow her iPad.

'Yes, but no games. It's not a toy.' She was always monitoring the children and how much time they spent on "gadgetry", as she called it. She wasn't part of the gaming generation, thought the children, otherwise she would have known that the interactive games they played were on their PC's, not on tablets. Mind you, ask their mother for a tablet and she would probably go to the bathroom cabinet!

In the warmth of the living room, Charlie and Lizzie got the search engine up and looked for "auction rooms close by". Being the only one in the vicinity, it came straight up with the site "wolfesauctions.co.uk".

'Here we go, Lizzie. Upcoming auctions. Next auction, January 17th.'

The website wasn't great, with everything randomly ordered, but there it was on Page 5 along with a photograph, "Lot 48: 17th Century Oak Refectory Dining Table". Result!

There wasn't much planning that needed doing, they just had to be opportunistic once they were there, coolly open the drawer and when nobody was watching give the false bottom a yank and grab the map. There would be no quick escape. They would have to sit through what was going to be, from then on, a very boring auction, particularly if any armchairs were being sold near the end and they had to wait for their father. Anyway, as long as they got it back, what difference was another hour going to make? For the time being, they contented themselves with thinking beyond the auction and what they should do once they had the map back in their possession.

Charlie and Lizzie spent the rest of the day keeping themselves busy, as they found that if they weren't doing anything, time passed at a snail's pace. They walked Glen, tidied their rooms, made everyone a cup of tea, put their bicycles away and even cleaned the car. To their surprise, they were so far into their parents' good books that their mother suggested they all go to the cinema for a treat.

'What would you like to see?'

'Any pirate films on?' asked Charlie.

'I'm not sure. Let me check.'

Sadly, there weren't, but they still spent a pleasant evening watching the latest children's blockbuster, "Gretlo".

Charlie and Lizzie yawned all the way home as the day's exertions caught up with them and once back at Granny's took themselves, much to their parents' delight, straight off to bed.

As the sun came up, Glen barked by the front door as usual. The children jumped out of bed and headed downstairs. They made themselves a cup of tea and started busying themselves about the house. At this stage of the game, they weren't leaving anything to chance. The one thing they didn't need was their parents telling them they didn't have time to go to the auction because there was "still too much to do".

After breakfast, it was just a case of walking Glen and making themselves useful. They spent most of the morning in relative silence. There was a lot on their minds, but little that needed talking about. The only thing they discussed briefly were their roles, which would be just as they had been at Wolfe Manor. Once Lizzie had the map, she would carefully fold it up and tuck it under her jumper. Then they would see the rest of the auction through, and only once they were home and in the safety of their bedroom, get the map out and give it a closer look. It was a simple plan, but simple plans are often the best.

There were jobs to do, and the morning passed quickly. With the auction starting at 2pm, Mrs Baldwin thought it an excellent idea if they ate at midday, an hour earlier than normal. It would be a pleasant distraction to get away for a while and do a little browsing.

Midday came, and the children ate their lunch in record time, followed by a frustratingly long wait for the big trip to town. A sense of excitement filled the air, even though they did their level best to contain it. They had the "essentials", most important of which was the Swiss Army knife. They would need that to lift the bottom of the drawer out.

'You children ready?' shouted Mr Baldwin. 'Can you shut Glen in the kitchen and jump in the car?'

At last they were off, heading back through the park and finally emerging from the gates into the outside world.

The auction looked like it was going to be busy judging by the lack of parking available nearby. Charlie and Lizzie audibly vented their frustration, huffing and puffing in the back as their father drove around in vain looking for a space, all the time getting further and further away. They finally parked "a short walk away" as Mr Baldwin put it. A short walk if you've got 50-foot-long legs, thought Charlie.

It was nippy outside, so the warmth of the auction rooms proved very welcome. Unlike the relative chaos of the website, the Wolfes had arranged the items incredibly well. Mr Baldwin barged past in a world of his own. He had spotted his first armchair. Much to his annoyance, someone else sat down in it just as he arrived, so he stood there, embarrassingly close, the children thought, until the lady vacated it. Mr Baldwin sat down and a smile came over his face. It was a beauty, leather covered, with signs of wear that looked very much in place for an obviously much used and loved piece of furniture. Then the debate started.

'It's amazingly comfortable.'

'It's huge. How on earth would we get it home? And it's tatty.'

'It's not tatty, just nicely worn. Have a sit in it.'

Mr Baldwin got up and made way for his wife.

'George, there's another one over there,' she said, trying her usual distraction technique.

'We're going to have a look around if that's ok?' said Charlie.

'Ok, just meet us back here ten minutes before the auction starts,' said Mr Baldwin.

The children shot off, eyes darting from left to right as they went.

'There it is!' squealed Lizzie in excitement, pointing to the other side of the room.

The children dashed to the table. It looked even better than they had remembered. No matter what anyone thought about the Wolfe brothers, they knew how to prepare things for auction. The table was beautifully clean and polished, but not overdone. In fact, it looked just right.

Lizzie felt under the end of the table for the drawer.

'Other end.'

In a flash, they were at the opposite end, but annoyingly, so were an elderly couple.

'Please go away,' said Charlie under his breath.

'Ooh, and there's a drawer down this end, that'll be useful,' said the woman, opening it, 'and it's a biggun too. Lot 48 Gareth, write that down.'

She almost trampled the children underfoot as she turned and walked away, without a word of apology. Bossy AND rude. Her poor husband, thought Charlie.

The children set to work. Charlie keeping a lookout whilst Lizzie opened the drawer. Once fully open, Lizzie got the penknife out of her pocket and, with the corkscrew attachment, wedged it into the gap at the back.

'It's stuck.'

Charlie looked in the drawer. 'Let me try.'

He pulled with all his might, almost falling over backwards as it finally came. To their horror, what they saw wasn't the map they had expected, but a photograph taken from a security camera showing the backs of two children and a dog. They were running across a lawn towards some woods. Underneath the photograph were the words "Look behind you".

Charlie and Lizzie's eyes widened as they looked at each other. Then slowly they turned their heads, and a terrifying sight met their gaze, for there stood one of the Wolfe brothers, his sinister appearance only broken by the slightest trace of a smile. He had now identified the children in the photograph.

Chapter 4:   A Shot in the Dark

The children left the auction in silence, shoulders slumped. The only thing that cheered them up even a little was their father's hilarious behaviour. He was in the most almighty grump because he'd yet again failed to buy a chair, made worse by his wife telling him not to act like a child. As their mother had proved once again, there was only one boss in this family!

Charlie spent the return journey deep in thought. The Wolfes had the map, with any chance of retrieving it now gone. All their excursion to Wolfe Manor had done was raise suspicions, which is undoubtedly why the Wolfes had given the table a good once over and eventually discovered the map. But no sense in crying over spilt milk. They needed a change of plan.

Once back at Granny's, Charlie grabbed his sister by the arm and led her upstairs. A few items of furniture remained, and the desk in their bedroom was one of them. Charlie lifted the top and took out the "Atlas of the World". He opened the front cover to reveal a near exact copy of the map. He lifted it out and plonked himself down on the bedroom floor with the map in front of him. Lizzy eased herself down by his side.

'What do you think?'

'I can't remember the map exactly, but it looks the same. When did you draw it?'

'Just after we lost the original, while it was still fresh in my mind. I've been mulling things over. Why did the Wolfes go to all the trouble of scaring us at the auction?'

'Do you think the map might be real and they know where the island is?'

'I'm certain it's genuine, and they obviously think so too. But it has so little detail. It'll be like looking for a needle in a haystack.' Charlie stared at the floor, an emptiness in his chest. Finally, he snapped out of it. Raising his head, he looked Lizzie in the eye. 'We might have lost Granny's map, but one thing's for sure, we won't lose her treasure, not if we can help it.'

The assurance in his voice lifted Lizzie's spirits. They would find the treasure, and before the Wolfes.

'Wait here, Lizzie.' Charlie jumped up and ran downstairs. Seconds later, he was back with their mother's iPad and sitting next to his sister.

To their frustration, the search for "Gravedigger's Bay" drew a blank.

'Ok, let's have an educated guess,' said Charlie.

'What do you mean?'

'It's a pirate's map as it had a Jolly Roger, and it was in our table, so we can safely assume that the pirate was from these shores.'

'Of course, the flag.' It hit her like a thunderbolt. 'Do you remember the pirate book we got for Christmas when we were small? It had loads of different flags and some pirates had their own special flag.'

'Well done, Lizzie.' Charlie tapped away at the screen. 'How about this one, "Pirate Flags From The Golden Age of Piracy"?'

A multitude of flags came up, all similar, but each in their own way unique. The children's eyes scanned the screen as fast as they could.

'Come on, keep scrolling,' said Lizzie.

'Check this one out,' pointed Charlie, 'smiling face, crossed cutlasses. It's almost identical. John Rackham, 1718.'

'Come on then. Who was John Rackham?' She was getting impatient.

'Here we are, "otherwise known as Calico Jack. Hanged and gibbeted in 1720, Port Royal, Jamaica". That's horrible. They just left him strung up as a warning to others. The good news is that it narrows it down a fair bit; let's see how many islands there are in the Caribbean. Oh great, 7000.'

'I'll grab Dad's iPad, then we can both search,' said Lizzie as she disappeared through the door.

Thirty seconds later, she was back sitting next to her brother.

'Right,' said Charlie, 'here's Jamaica. I'll go north and you head south.'

'Dinner, everyone,' their mother called up the stairs.

Once they were sitting at the table, Mr Baldwin made an announcement.

'Children, your mother and I have been talking. It's been tough for us all recently, what with Granny and everything, so once we've finished sorting things out, we should go on a really special holiday for a couple of weeks. We all need some time off and a change of environment would do us all the world of good. How do you feel about South Africa? It'll be nice and hot at this time of year.'

'Or the Caribbean,' said Lizzie, quick as a flash.

'We don't mind where we go,' said Mrs Baldwin, her face beaming as she sat there, taking in every word. 'The key thing is that we'll all be together and able to relax in the sun. Let's put the Caribbean on the shortlist. Did you have anywhere particular in mind?'

'We don't have to decide now,' said Mr Baldwin. 'Let's all sleep on it and continue the discussion in the morning.'

This suited the children down to the ground, and no sooner had they finished their dinner than they were back upstairs continuing their search.

'I'm doing the Bahamas now. What about you Lizzie?'

'I've been going slowly so I won't miss anything. I don't want to do this all again.'

'Don't worry, I'm being careful too.'

Lizzie gave a sharp intake of breath. 'I think I've found it.' She looked from the iPad to the drawing and then back again. 'But the bay doesn't have a name.'

Charlie was by her side in an instant. She was right. It was almost identical. The only thing that troubled him was that it was a long way from Jamaica. It was a shot in the dark, but it was all they had. Now came the problem of how to get there. It was small, too small for an airport surely, but as they zoomed in, there it was, with a single runway.

'It's not quite Heathrow, but it'll do,' said Charlie.

The next morning, when Mr Baldwin broached the subject of holidays, the children were ready.

'We've been looking at the Caribbean more closely,' said Charlie, 'and we thought a holiday on a small island might be just the thing we all need. We could relax, read, explore, snorkel. It would feel like a world away from here.'

'We've done some research and found a group of islands that look fantastic,' said Lizzie. 'One of them's amazing. It only has the tiniest of airports, so it will be pretty unspoilt. We'd have to fly to Barbados first and go on from there.'

'It all sounds quite expensive,' said Mrs Baldwin, whose tone of voice made it abundantly clear that she wasn't over the moon about the idea. 'Wouldn't you like to do something more exciting than just sit in the sun?'

But something had tweaked Mr Baldwin's interest and a smile lit up his face. 'I don't know, it's worth looking into.'

After breakfast, Mr and Mrs Baldwin went for a walk with Glen. For once, they weren't insistent that the children join them, a sure sign that they wanted to talk amongst themselves. When they got back, both had the same rather inane grin on their face.

'Right children,' said Mr Baldwin as they gathered in the kitchen, 'we've decided. Let's do it. Your mother and I will research how we get there and hunt for accommodation this afternoon. If it all looks ok, then we'll go over half term.'

'But that's in February,' said Charlie. 'Do we really have to wait until then?' If they had found the island, so might the Wolfe brothers. If this was the case, he didn't want to hang around any longer than necessary. 'It's been a traumatic time for all of us. Shouldn't we go as soon as possible?'

'I'll not hear another word about it,' said Mr Baldwin. 'School will keep your mind on other things until then. Anyway, we are doing this as much for your mother as anyone else and we've both agreed on half term.'

The children begrudgingly agreed. After all, it was only four weeks away.

Back in their own home, they used the weeks productively, researching the island as much as they could. With a pretty good idea of what lay in store for them, they came up with a basic plan of attack and a list of things to take.

Not for one instant did the children contemplate failure, which was odd given the circumstances. They had lost the original map, a map with very little detail. Hopefully, they had identified the right island, although there was no reference to Gravedigger's Bay anywhere. They didn't know what they were after or if it was of any value, and they didn't know where exactly to start. Other than that, everything was perfect. As Charlie kept reminding Lizzie, even with all these things stacked against them, it was still better odds than winning the lottery!

With school and planning for their adventure, the children had become oblivious to everything going on around them. Had this not been the case, they might have noticed their father's rather strange behaviour. He had been telephoning and visiting a lot of relatives, which, although not entirely out of the ordinary, would have made them very suspicious had they noticed that whenever they were nearby, he would either speak in a whisper or not at all. He was becoming very occupied with something, and from the way he was acting, increasingly excited to boot. There were constant trips to the workshop and banging late into the night. A continuous stream of tiny packages arrived daily in the post. Then there were the drawers in his study, normally accessible to all, but now under permanent lock and key.

Charlie and Lizzie were busy with their own agenda. They had the essentials, to which they added notebooks, pens, and following their online investigations, a small handsaw, a hammer, a handful of nails and a folding shovel their father had rather conveniently brought back from Granny's. There were a lot more things they had discussed taking, but they needed to be smart. They didn't want their bags to be so heavy as to arouse suspicion. Anyway, they had their holiday stuff to take, too.

With one day to go, the doorbell rang. Charlie answered the front door to the postman, who had been trying to get a ridiculously large envelope through the letterbox. He handed it to Charlie, who took it through to the kitchen and plonked it on the table. Addressed to his father and with "Jones Engineering" stamped on the front, it looked like more boring work stuff.

With all the excitement of the holiday, the day passed quickly, and it was soon time for bed. Lizzie sauntered upstairs whilst Charlie went to find their parents to say goodnight. As he wandered towards the kitchen, the first thing he noticed was the door firmly shut. Something wasn't right. He crept up and put his ear to the door.

'Will we have to move?' asked Mrs Baldwin.

'I think we might have to.'

'To a smaller house? I don't know if I could.'

Charlie didn't understand. Then he realised. The letter. His father had lost his job. Charlie's heart sank. He felt empty inside. They knew he hated change. Then a lightbulb came on in his head. The treasure. He wasn't going to find it for Granny, but for the entire family. For the time being, he'd keep it to himself. He needed to think.

The next morning and with bags packed, the Baldwin family set off for the airport.

'I'm surprised we've got so much luggage,' said Mr Baldwin, grinning away.

The children smiled back nervously. With any luck, he was just trying to make their mother aware that she always took too much on holiday. She carried on reading, completely oblivious to all conversation. She always took an armful of holiday books with her, which she started as soon as they stepped outside the front door.

There wasn't much excitement on the initial leg of the journey, other than Charlie and Lizzie realising they could order fizzy drinks on the plane and not even have to pay for them. This was the life they thought, free drinks, free food and goodness knows how many films to watch on the little screen in front of you.

On arrival in Barbados, there was just enough time for a quick trip to the beach and a swim before their connecting flight. The sea was so warm it felt like they'd only been in a few minutes before it was time to get dressed again and head back to the airport.

The children were ready in an instant. There were important things to be getting on with. There was a definite air of excitement until they saw the plane they were about to board. It was, shall we say, rather smaller than they had envisaged.

'Look on the bright side,' said Mr Baldwin, 'at least it has TWO propellers!

Chapter 5:   Welcome to the Caribbean

The flight was rather fun, for most of them, anyway. Few of the creature comforts you get with normal aircraft, but far more exciting. Charlie and Lizzie loved it, bobbing up and down with every gust and their father counting the islands as they passed by. Had he looked the other way, he would have noticed that his wife, now white as a sheet, had put down her book.

The aircraft was small, so small in fact that it should have been no surprise to anyone when they were told that one of their bags would be on the next flight. Apparently, there wasn't enough room in the hold for it this time. Of course, it was the one that Charlie and Lizzie had their equipment in, but there wasn't anything they could do, so they bit their lips. The baggage handler, who was also the pilot, told Mr Baldwin that they would bring it directly to their hotel when it arrived.

The hotel was another source of excitement, as Mrs Baldwin had arranged the accommodation and kept it secret. She grabbed a pen and paper from her bag, wrote the address down, and gave it to the pilot.

'Is it walking distance?' Mr Baldwin asked his wife. 'Or do we need a taxi?'

'It should be about ten minutes by taxi. Everyone take a bag and we'll go out the front and grab one.'

They hadn't realised that small airports on small islands have very few taxis, so although there was a sign outside saying "Taxi Rank", there wasn't a car in sight.

'There's a telephone number under the sign,' said Charlie.

They wandered across and put their bags down and Mr Baldwin got out his phone and dialled.

'Right, it won't be long. He just has to finish his beer, then he'll be here. Not quite the big city!'

Charlie and Lizzie, never having been anywhere quite like this before, found the unfamiliar surroundings mesmerising. The palm trees swayed in the sea breeze, while brightly-coloured birds squawked as they flitted from tree to tree. The empty roads meant that the sound of cicadas replaced the usual hum of traffic. Lizzie pointed to an enormous bright green lizard enjoying the sunshine. It watched them unblinkingly as they approached. A car came around the corner, diverting their gaze momentarily. When they looked back, it had vanished.

'Greetings,' said the driver, getting out of the car, 'my name's Tallboy.' He wasn't wrong, he must have been nearly seven feet tall, but skinny as a rake.

The car itself would have been quite roomy, but that was without Tallboy driving. His legs were so long that most of him seemed to be seated in the back with the Baldwin family.

'Welcome to the Caribbean,' he said, having wasted no time in getting the luggage into the back. 'Where can I take you?'

'The Grand Hotel please,' said Mrs Baldwin with a smile.

'The Grand coming right up.' They pulled away, slowly. The children were enjoying the apparent laid-back life of the Caribbean.

The journey would have been a lot quicker if Tallboy hadn't insisted on talking the entire time, giving them a guided tour of the south coast of the island at a rather leisurely fifteen miles an hour. It made Mr Baldwin question, rather too loudly the children thought, whether the car had more than two forward gears. But Tallboy wasn't listening. He was far too fond of the sound of his own voice.

'Here we are, The Grand. Shall I take your bags in?'

Mr Baldwin looked at the meter and got out his wallet. 'We'll be fine with the bags, thanks. Here you go, keep the change.'

With a casual salute and a smile of appreciation, Tallboy got back in the car. He held a card out through the window.

'Here's my number if you need me again. Have a wonderful holiday, and mind the sharks,' he joked.

Just as the children were about to enter the hotel, Mrs Baldwin called out to them. 'No, we're over here.'

Directly opposite The Grand Hotel stood the less salubrious Betty's Guesthouse.

'Don't worry, I read all the reviews and they say it's friendly, exceptionally clean, with amazing food.'

'And I bet I know who wrote the reviews.' Mr Baldwin stopped talking instantly upon seeing the rather withering glance from his wife.

40

As was so often the case, Mrs Baldwin, not so annoyingly in this instance, proved to be correct. Although rather shabby looking from the outside, Betty's Guesthouse had a homely feel and was spotlessly clean.

The man standing behind the reception desk was in his late forties and, by the look of the stretched buttons on his chef's whites, enjoyed his own cooking a little too much. His cheerful demeanour and broad grin couldn't hide a natural air of authority which more than made up for his lack of stature. With his short black hair and spotlessly clean clothes, he was a man who knew his business.

'Welcome. You must be the Baldwin family. I'm Burty, this is my place.'

'But I thought the sign said Betty's Guesthouse,' said Mr Baldwin, looking puzzled.

'That's what happens when you employ someone you think is 90% sign-writer and 10% village idiot and they turn out to be 10% sign-writer and 90% village idiot.'

Burty grabbed a couple of bags and showed the Baldwins to their small but comfortable adjoining rooms. Perfect, thought the children.

Everyone was feeling the effects of a long day. It was only 6pm on the island, but that meant 10pm in the UK.

'How about a quick bite to eat, then bed?' said Mr Baldwin. 'We want to be fresh for tomorrow.'

The children didn't argue; they knew they needed their wits about them. They had a lot of digging around to do, in every sense!

Charlie and Lizzie awoke at 6:30 the next morning, with the sun coming up over the horizon. It was too early to wake their parents, so they got showered and dressed and Charlie made himself a cup of tea. Lizzie wasn't a great fan of tea, so made do with a glass of water.

'Urghhh,' said Charlie as he took his first sip of Caribbean herbal tea with long life milk. It wasn't quite like being back home. But he struggled on, being too lazy, or as he would say, "tired" at this hour of the morning, to get up and exchange it for something else.

By the door, they spotted the missing suitcase that their father had deposited the previous evening. They opened it and dug out the handsaw, hammer, some nails and the folding shovel. To this they added their towels, masks, snorkels and the essentials, popping it all in their rucksacks. Charlie was careful to split everything 50:50 to avoid any moaning from his younger sibling.

'Let's see if we can find someone and get a map of the island,' said Lizzie.

It was still only just after 7:30, and they hadn't heard a sound from next door. It would be at least another half an hour before their parents were ready to go anywhere, so they might as well use the time constructively.

'Good idea. Let's try the restaurant first. I'm sure we'll find someone there.'

As they walked in, they saw a tall, slender lady in a strikingly colourful dress gliding from table to table.

'Good morning, my name is Sandra. What can I get you?'

'We're still waiting for our parents to get up so will have breakfast later if that's ok,' said Lizzie. 'Actually, we were wondering where we could find a map of the island.'

'You children come with me.'

Sandra, closely followed by Charlie and Lizzie, made her way towards the reception area. The children hadn't noticed it when they arrived, probably as there was so much else to take in, but there was a small rack of leaflets showing various things to do and places to visit on the island. If the meagre number of leaflets was anything to go by, there wasn't that much to do at all.

'Here you go,' she said, handing Charlie a brochure with a map on the back.

'Thank you, Sandra. See you later.'

They went back to their room and spread the disappointingly small map on the floor. The island looked tiny. It had few proper roads, everywhere being connected by a spider's web of tracks and paths. It made sense, the more remote places didn't even look reachable by vehicle.

The map might have been small, but the one thing it did show were place names, and there it was, in big letters, Whaler's Bay.

Charlie and Lizzie looked at each other, and for the first time, genuine doubt crept in. According to the

43

map they had seen at Granny's, this should have been Gravedigger's Bay, not Whaler's Bay. Charlie's map looked just like the island, but there must be millions of islands around the world, seven thousand in the Caribbean alone. Charlie felt his stomach tie itself up in a knot.

Their gazes locked on the map, willing it to change. But the more they stared, the bigger the letters got, WHALER'S BAY, until it was all they saw, everything around it fading into oblivion.

The entire trip had been a complete waste of time. Worse than that, they were going to lose the house, their home. Even though their parents were unaware of what they had been up to, Charlie felt like he and Lizzie had let them both down terribly. There was nothing to say, so they sat there in silence.

Finally, Charlie snapped out of it.

'Look on the bright side, it's going to save us a heap of digging.'

Lizzie smiled, but she could tell from the tone of Charlie's voice that he, like her, knew the game was over.

'And I bet there's some fantastic snorkelling. Have you seen the water? It's crystal clear.'

The sound of movement next door broke the sombre mood. At last, their parents were awake. Now just the usual thirty minutes for them to make themselves presentable. What was it with parents that meant they had to take so long getting up? Not only pointless, but blooming annoying.

'You children up?' shouted Mrs Baldwin. 'Breakfast in twenty minutes.'

'Up and dressed,' said Charlie.

They lay there on their beds chatting and thinking about what might have been.

'You never know,' said Lizzie, 'we might find something else,' but she knew in her heart that the real fun was over. It was still going to be a glorious holiday though, just a more normal one.

There was a knock on the door as their parents entered the room, and they headed off for breakfast.

As they arrived at the restaurant, it surprised their parents when Sandra, who was in fact both the waitress and breakfast chef, greeted the children like long-lost friends.

'What can I get you? Muesli, fresh fruit, fried bakes.' Fried bakes, as she then explained, were like doughnuts, but much better, and it was quite normal to have them for breakfast.

After a hearty breakfast that included almost everything on offer, they headed back to their rooms to collect the gear. On the way, they bumped into Burty, who acknowledged them with a big smile.

'Good morning, and where are you all going today?'

'We fancied a bit of snorkelling.' said Mr Baldwin. 'Any recommendations where to go?'

'Whaler's Bay is always good and not too far. But don't dig down too deep. You never know what you might find. They used to call it Gravedigger's Bay,' he said, chuckling to himself. 'They changed the name some years ago, so it didn't scare the tourists.' He thought this was extremely amusing. What he hadn't noticed was the excitement on Charlie's and Lizzie's faces.

Chapter 6:   A Day of Adventure

'So why Gravedigger's Bay?' asked Mrs Baldwin. She had inherited many of her mother's traits, one of which was an appetite for the not so normal.

'As the story goes, a long, long time ago a pirate ship went aground not far offshore in a storm. They imagined themselves lucky as it blew over without loss of life, but unable to re-float the ship, the crew came ashore. Soon the first few people became ill, vomiting and bleeding. Slowly but surely, they all succumbed to what they later put down to a terrible strain of dengue fever, carried by the mosquitoes. Only a handful of the crew survived, and whether it was the pirate code or they were just being Christian, they buried every one of their lost crewmates. Nobody knew the names of the survivors, although there were rumours that one of them was Calico Jack himself. Afterwards, it became known as Gravedigger's Bay. More recently, they changed the name to Whaler's Bay. It's where the old whalers holed up during storms when they were out after humpbacks.'

Charlie and Lizzie's eyes shot out on stalks. First Gravedigger's Bay, now Calico Jack!

'Come on, we've got fish to fry,' said Charlie. 'All we need are our bags. Lizzie and I got a map of the island this morning. Look, Whaler's Bay. We could even walk if we can't get a taxi.'

Normally the children would have held out for a taxi, but goodness knows if Tallboy was even out of bed at this hour of the morning. It would probably be quicker to walk.

The tracks were easy to follow, but rougher going than expected, so it was half an hour before they finally arrived at the beach. But the time passed quickly, as the conversation turned to pirates.

'What a load of old twaddle,' said Mr Baldwin. 'Gravedigger's Bay and Calico Jack, I imagine someone's been watching too much "Pirates of the Caribbean". And bodies buried all over the place, really, a great story for the tourists, but you would have hoped they could have come up with something better than that. Buried treasure, now that WOULD be a tourist attraction.'

Charlie nudged his sister on the arm and smiled. Everything made perfect sense. The only question he had was what on earth it was that they were looking for. Would they recognise it if they even found it? Perhaps all the map showed was the location of the graveyard.

'Well, I thought it was an interesting story,' said Mrs Baldwin. 'There were lots of buccaneers in those days. Of course, the story would have become exaggerated over the years, but that's perfectly normal. I find it quite exciting just being here now.'

As soon as they had laid out their towels, Charlie grabbed Lizzie by the arm and they headed off to do their first recce of the area. The sun was already high in the sky and after twenty minutes the heat was getting to them, so Lizzie suggested a quick swim.

Charlie needed little encouragement and seconds later, they shot past their parents towards the sea.

'Watch out for sharks,' said Mrs Baldwin, remembering what Tallboy had said.

Charlie turned and gave his mother a withering look. That wasn't funny at all; she knew he had a thing about sharks.

Mr Baldwin grabbed the masks and snorkels and joined them, and they spent the next twenty minutes in silence, floating around the bay admiring the strikingly colourful fish.

Back on the beach, Charlie and Lizzie announced they were going to continue exploring. Not before they had put on some suntan lotion, said their mother, looking at their backs.

The bay itself was crescent-shaped and covered by fine white sand. It was larger than it looked on the map and bordered entirely by trees on the landward side. Other than the track leading down to the beach, there were no signs of civilisation. Being sandwiched between the sea on one side and the trees on the other, it had a secluded, natural and untouched feel about it. It wouldn't have been so very different all those years ago when the crew made it ashore, thought Lizzie. It must have seemed like paradise before the fever struck.

'Did you see that?' said Charlie in a half whisper.

'No, what was it?'

'Something in the trees over there,' he said, pointing.

'Where abouts?'

'Don't worry, it was probably just a shadow. Let's keep going.'

The initial reconnaissance finished, the children returned to their towels for a drink. Now they knew what lay in store, they could start planning for tomorrow. Whatever they were looking for had been there for hundreds of years, so it was unlikely to disappear overnight.

'I just saw someone,' said Lizzie, looking beyond Charlie to the trees.

'Someone?'

'Yes, there was a scrawny-looking man in the trees. He was watching us. When he saw me looking at him, he ran away.'

'Scrawny, anything else?'

'I only glimpsed him for a second, but if you asked me to describe him, I would say "think Robinson Crusoe".'

Charlie scanned the woods. It must have been the same person he'd spotted before. One thing bothered him, though. Why on earth should someone be watching them?

Once their parents got back to their towels, the children told them about the man in the woods. Their father asked everyone to remain vigilant and suggested someone stay with the bags at all times. This suited Mrs Baldwin perfectly. She could sit under the parasol with one of her books without a care in the world.

When they arrived back at the guesthouse later that afternoon, Mr Baldwin thought he should mention the man in the trees to Burty. He might well know something.

'Ah yes, you don't want to go worrying yourselves about old Catweazle. He's been there for years, lives in a small shack somewhere in the woods. He keeps himself to himself, seems to like it that way. We always say, "if you don't bother him, he won't bother you".'

'Catweazle, that was a television series back in the 1970s,' said Mrs Baldwin.

'That's where he got the nickname from. I've never seen it, but apparently he looks just like him.'

'So we've got nothing to worry about?'

'Not at all, he just likes to monitor things, from a distance, of course. He stays well out of the way most of the time.'

'Well, children, you heard that. Try to pretend he's not there. Anyway, we can try a different beach tomorrow.'

Back in their room, Charlie pulled the notebook from his rucksack and plonked it on the table by the window. He sat down and Lizzie pulled the other chair around beside him. He'd already put pen to paper and mapped out the area and was now busy splitting it into sections.

'We can cross off each section as we make our way along the beach.'

'So where shall we start?' asked Lizzie.

'We have to imagine what the pirates would have done. If it was heavy, they wouldn't have carried it far, so just off the beach is where we should

51

concentrate our efforts,' he said, tapping the pencil on the drawing. 'As for where along the beach, your guess is as good as mine.'

'In the middle, then?'

'As good a place as any. We can start there, then work one way a little and then the other.'

'How are we going to do it? We can't just start digging up the entire beach, it will take forever.'

'I've already thought about that,' said Charlie, turning to face his sister. 'Have you seen how they look for people after an avalanche? They use long poles and push them deep into the snow to see if they hit anything solid.'

'OK, go on.'

'The sand in the bay, it's very fine. If we can find something similar, then we can poke down into the sand every six inches until we hit something solid. It'll take time, but so be it.'

'So we need to find something long and thin.'

'Yes, and strong, we don't want it breaking on us.'

Lizzie thought it was a great idea, but there was no way she was going to tell her brother that. It was still going to take an awfully long time, but at least there'd be no digging until absolutely necessary, and that suited her down to the ground.

As they finished their discussion, there was a knock on the adjoining door.

'You children coming for a drink before dinner? We thought we might try the terrace at The Grand. It looks quite nice,' said Mr Baldwin.

'OK,' said Charlie.

'See you outside in five minutes.'

Planning done, Charlie and Lizzie put on their shorts and t-shirts and waited outside. The only thing left now was making sure they ended up at Gravedigger's Bay again tomorrow.

On their way through reception, they bumped into Burty, so Mr Baldwin told him they would be back later for dinner.

As they walked into the entrance hall of The Grand, it was like being in a different world. The circular atrium, with pristine white walls, glass domed roof, and enormous pots containing palm trees, lent it an outdoor feel. Small brightly coloured birds filled the entire place with birdsong, as they flitted continually from inside to out through the large doors leading to the terrace.

'Can I help you?' came a voice to their left. They spun round to see an impeccably dressed young man.

'We'd like to have a drink,' said Mr Baldwin.

'Follow me, please Sir, Madam,' he said, leading them out to a table on the terrace.

As they walked through the doors, the first thing that hit them was the spectacular view. They were looking over a small bay with its own beach, and in it were a dozen small fishing boats and yachts. There was a slight breeze, so the boats danced on their moorings, masts swaying from side to side. There was a rather old looking blue and white wooden boat, dragged onto the beach, and beside it stood a man fiddling with his nets. Way in the distance, they could see a cruise ship crossing from left to right. The island was too small and so of little interest to such a large vessel.

They sat down in their chairs and ordered two rum punches and two lemonades, which promptly arrived accompanied by a bowl of assorted nuts.

'This is the life,' said Mrs Baldwin.

'It is indeed,' came a voice from behind them.

They turned to see the tall and, even in this setting, rather frightening looking figures of the Wolfe brothers.

Chapter 7:   The Competition Begins

'Well, you could knock me down with a feather,' said Mr Baldwin. 'What a surprise. Imagine, of all the places in the world. What brings you here?'

'The same as you I would have thought,' said Peregrine (or was it Edward) Wolfe, a knowing smile on his face. 'The tranquility and the weather.'

Charlie and Lizzie sat there in silence, stone-faced, as the brothers sidled over, towering above them.

'Are you staying at The Grand too?'

'No, we're staying across the road,' said Mrs Baldwin, looking up. 'We've come here for an apéritif.'

'Ah, the guesthouse, yes. It looks very, how shall I say, good value.'

'It's extremely comfortable and from what we've eaten so far, the food's fantastic. You should try it,' she replied, not liking the tone of his voice.

'Hmm, yes. Well, don't let us detain you any longer. Have a lovely holiday.'

'You too, and no doubt see you again,' replied Mr Baldwin.

'Undoubtedly,' he said, turning to face the children and giving them a chilling glance before heading to the door.

As soon as they were out of earshot, the parents' conversation quickly turned to the Wolfes. They really were the last people you could ever imagine being in the Caribbean. They just didn't fit. Pasty white, probably not a pair of swimming trunks between them; or even a pair of shorts, they joked.

Charlie and Lizzie, making sure they laughed in all the right bits, said nothing.

After their drinks, they got up and walked back across the road for dinner, but not before having a quick peek at the menu in The Grand.

'Expensive, but it looks good; perhaps we'll come and eat here for a change one evening,' said Mr Baldwin.

Back at the guesthouse, they tucked into their meals, but it seemed, as the evening wore on, that they were all on autopilot. It had been an active day, what with the trek to and from the beach and a day in the sun. As is so often the case, tiredness hits you most when you relax.

It wasn't long before they were in their rooms, lights out, the children quietly discussing the plans for the next day. The Wolfe brothers were close on their heels, so the operation required extra care and putting into action immediately. Their avalanche search technique was ideal as it would leave little trace. But the Wolfes would be following their every move, just as they would be the Wolfes.

One thing had slipped their minds. Catweazle would be close by monitoring everyone.

As the sun came up over the horizon, the children awoke to a slight commotion that had started outside on the road. With the four-hour time difference between the UK and Caribbean, just as it was proving difficult to stay awake in the evenings, so it was proving very easy to get up at the crack of dawn.

'We are not paying you a penny unless you have ALL the gear,' said one of the Wolfes. 'We have a plan to stick to and we've told you what we need, so just get us what we've asked for.'

'But it will be dangerous, even if nobody breaks anything, there is no way they won't get hurt. Anyway, where can I get things like that on this island?'

'I don't care where you get them from, just get them; or make them if you have to. We can do without people snooping around trying to see what we're up to. Of course, we don't want to hurt anyone,' he said in a far less aggressive tone. 'We merely want to know if anyone is becoming overly interested in what we are doing. They're a deterrent, really.'

The children listened intently. It sounded like things were hotting up. One thing was certain, they had better keep an eye out for anything untoward in the woods.

'I hope they're not talking about mantraps. They can break your leg,' said Charlie, his imagination now running wild. He couldn't believe that anyone, even the Wolfes, would resort to such things. They had banned mantraps in most countries years ago.

Charlie and Lizzie were dying to tell their parents what had just been said and voice their concerns, but it would only lead to a lot of unwanted questions, which they could rather do without. They might let them know what was going on when the time was right, but not until then. They didn't want to look foolish and make their parents think they had come all this way on a wild goose chase.

It was still early, so once the disturbance outside had stopped, the children waited for a couple of minutes for the coast to clear before venturing outside.

'Right Lizzie, you know what sort of thing we're looking for?'

'Yep, something long and thin to push into the sand.'

'And strong. We don't want them breaking. It'll be a heck of a trip back to get new ones.'

Everything they picked up was too flimsy or too flexible. Although it had sounded like a good idea, not finding anything was becoming rather frustrating.

Just as they had all but given up hope of finding anything up to the task, Charlie spotted something on a building site on the opposite side of the road.

'Hey, Lizzie, over there.'

They sidled across the road and Charlie pointed to a heap of builder's rubbish. There, amongst the empty cement bags and offcuts of wood, were several rather rusty looking metal rods.

'They look like just the job,' said Charlie, 'see if you can find any which are a decent length.'

'They're blooming heavy. I don't know if I fancy lugging one of these to the beach every day. Can we try to find something lighter?'

'These'll do just fine. Anyway, we'll only have to take them there once. We can hide them by the beach after that.'

Lizzie couldn't argue. They were exactly what they'd been looking for, and after a bit of digging around in the pile, they found a couple which looked ideal.

Minutes later, they were back at Burty's. They hid the two metal rods behind a bush and returned to their room. As they walked in, their rather irate mother was there to greet them.

'Where have you two been? We've been calling for you for ages.'

'Sorry, Mum,' said Lizzie, 'we woke up early and went for a walk so you could have a lie in.'

'Well, please don't do it again. What's that on your hands?'

The children hadn't noticed it before, but their hands were bright orange with rust.

'You'd better give them a jolly good wash before breakfast,' she carried on. 'Right, we'll see you over there in five minutes.'

When they arrived for breakfast, the children mentioned nothing of the morning's goings on. They just sat there, with clean hands, as good as gold, tucking into their fried bakes.

With breakfast finished, the deliberations about what to do that day began. Mrs Baldwin wanted to climb to the highest point on the island, whilst her husband wanted to go fishing. After a five-minute debate involving sea-sickness and the overpowering heat, they left the decision to the children. Charlie and Lizzie had only one place on their minds. Gravedigger's Bay it was.

Mrs Baldwin decided she should try to find the local supermarket, so she made her way to Reception. Burty pointed her towards Eglit's Emporium. Emporium, she thought, that sounded promising. That was, until she entered the shop and saw it was about the same size as a large caravan. Looks can be deceptive, and the more she looked around, the more she saw. In no time at all, she had an old cardboard box filled to the brim with bread, cheese, a few snacks, and some drinks. That's enough, she thought. After all, they still had to carry it to the beach.

Mrs Baldwin rang the bell at the checkout to get some attention, and no sooner had she done so than a sprightly 70-year-old came through the back door. He was of average height and very skinny, the well-defined muscles in his arms and legs telling the story of an active life. He had a kind face and his manner said that his grey hair was due to age, not stress.

'You must be Eglit?' she asked.

'No ma'am, that's my grandfather. He gets rather tired these days, so leaves the running of the shop to me.'

'Your grandfather, but he must…'

'be 110 ma'am. My name's Vin.'

'Well Vin, if I could pay for these, please.'

'Yes, ma'am.'

Much to her surprise, it turned out to be astonishingly good value. As she left, she said a cheery goodbye to Vin and assured him he would be seeing rather a lot of her and her family over the coming fortnight.

Once back at the guesthouse and with everything packed, they set off for the beach, with one minor detour via the bush to pick up their metal rods.

'What on earth are you going to do with those?' asked Mr Baldwin.

'We thought we'd try to do some treasure hunting in the bay. You never know what you might find if pirates have been there,' replied Charlie.

'A load of old bones, from what Burty said. Let's hope they're not contagious,' he said, grinning from ear to ear.

Both parents were more than happy that Charlie and Lizzie had got their way with a day at the beach. It would have seemed an eternity if the children had got bored and started moaning. Anyway, sunbathing, swimming, eating and reading; it wasn't a bad way to spend a day. They were on holiday, after all.

As they drew off the track and through the trees onto the beach, they heard voices and realised that the tranquility of the previous day was going to be hard to come by.

At the far right-hand end of the beach, the Wolfes were barking orders at a couple of locals.

Chapter 8: Eyes Everywhere

Lizzie wished she'd brought a camera. The brothers looked absolutely hilarious. They were wearing rather formal white shirts, which they had tried to make appear more casual by pulling the sleeves up. And what first appeared as dark shorts, on closer inspection, turned out to be their long black trousers rolled up to the knees. Add to this their short black socks and there they stood, two men, somehow magically transported from a funeral in North Wales to a beach in the Caribbean, without a change of attire!

They weren't hanging about, though. Their two new employees were already busy marking out areas in the sand with sticks. One brother glanced across and spotted the Baldwins. All went momentarily silent, then both parties acknowledged each other with a wave, before the Wolfes carried on, this time in much quieter tones.

The children looked at each other. The Wolfes must have come to the same conclusion as them, meaning that time was of the essence. At least they were in different parts of the bay, but Charlie and Lizzie had to work fast.

The one thing neither party had noticed, as they were paying far too much attention to each other, was the slow but steady movement in the trees. Catweazle was used to being on his own, and he didn't object to the occasional family who made the long trek to the bay in search of peace. This time, it was different.

There were far too many people on the beach and they weren't acting like holidaymakers. He stopped and stood there motionless amongst the undergrowth; watching.

With the Wolfes busying themselves on their part of the beach, the Baldwin family walked a little further than they had done the previous day. The children resisted going too far though, the one thing they didn't want was to be right at the far end. They had to start their search nearer the middle to give themselves the best chance of success.

'Can we stop here?' asked Lizzie. 'I'm boiling, and the water looks so inviting.'

'OK,' replied Mr Baldwin, 'this will do. Can one of you children put the cool bag under a tree? I can't imagine it's going to go anywhere.'

Charlie grabbed the bag and stuck it under the nearest tree, before running into the sea to join his sister for some snorkelling. A couple of minutes later and impatient to get going, Charlie tapped her on the back.

'Come on Lizzie, we've got work to do.'

Their father couldn't help smiling as they announced they were off in search of treasure, rods in hand.

'We need stones or sticks, Lizzie, so we can mark out our first area.'

There weren't many things lying around, but the children soon found four decent sized bits of driftwood, which they set out in a square measuring 5 paces by 5.

'OK, let's work our way westwards, moving away from the Wolfes. Remember, the first two sticks are in line with that rock next to the palm tree,' Charlie said, pointing.

A static reference would be ideal, he thought. It must have survived hurricanes in the past, so wasn't going anywhere in a hurry and should be immune from outside interference.

Within the square, Lizzie started at the side closest to the trees and Charlie nearest the sea. The sand was fine and loosely bound to the seaward side, so Charlie made quick work of it. For Lizzie, it proved an entirely different kettle of fish, as not only was the sand more compacted, but there were roots to deal with too. The first one she hit caused a great deal of excitement until they dug deeper and found out what it was. This was going to take longer than they had originally planned.

Twenty minutes later, and with two quadrants done, the children were sweltering and extremely bored.

'Swim?' said Charlie.

'Good idea.'

'Find anything?' asked their mother as they approached.

'Nothing yet,' replied Lizzie, 'but we'll keep on trying. Rome wasn't built in a day.'

Their parents stared at each other in astonishment. Was this really one of their children talking? They had never shown patience like that before.

'Must have hit her head on something,' said Mr Baldwin.

It was coming up to midday, so having all been in for a cooling dip, they sat down for lunch. The children are ravenous, thought Mrs Baldwin, as she watched them shovelling the food into their mouths. Within ten minutes of starting lunch, they were up, resuming their search.

A flash from the other end of the beach grabbed Charlie and Lizzie's attention, and both looked around simultaneously. They strained their eyes, only to see the Wolfe brothers, way in the distance. One of them was sitting under a parasol in a deckchair. That wasn't a problem; what the children didn't like was that the deckchair was facing them, and the man sitting on it had his binoculars trained directly on them. The sun flashed once again on the lens, and Lizzie looked at Charlie.

'We should have brought binoculars too.'

'We couldn't bring everything. Anyway, we weren't to know.'

'They're miles away. How are we going to keep an eye on them?'

'There's only one way, get closer. We can take it in turns. I'll go first.'

'You don't think it'll be too dangerous? Remember what you said about mantraps.'

'We'll be ok. It's daytime and we'll just need to keep our eyes peeled. You carry on here and I'll do the first check.'

Charlie disappeared into the trees, moving in silence on the sandy ground. He hadn't felt nervous before, but now he had butterflies in his stomach and his heart was pounding like a drum. The adrenalin amplified every sound, making it difficult to concentrate. With his bare feet, he crept along, making sure before every step that the ground was clear. Now only 30 yards from the beach, he could see them almost perfectly. The two muscle-bound assistants worked relentlessly, digging one trench after another. They intrigued Charlie; he needed to see more. Ever so slowly, he continued forward. The one to the left turned to face him, and Charlie froze. His chest was criss-crossed with scars, the like of which Charlie had never seen before. His colleague glanced up and Charlie swallowed hard. What had happened to his right eye?

The men resumed their digging and Charlie moved closer, mesmerised. His focus momentarily elsewhere, he yelped as he stubbed his toe on an old tree root.

The men stopped, turning towards the trees. Charlie wanted to scream, but stayed motionless behind a palm, waiting for the pain to subside.

'Who's there? You two, go into the woods and see who it is,' ordered one of the Wolfes.

The two men dropped their tools and raced towards the sound, crashing through everything in their path. Petrified, Charlie found himself unable to move. The footsteps came closer and closer until he heard their heavy breath only feet away. A loud crack 10 yards to his left captured everyone's attention, and the men turned to see the leathery back of a man wearing some rather ragged shorts. He was running away and not looking back.

The men shouted at him before turning and walking back towards the beach.

'It was only Catweazle, boss. He lives in these parts in a shack in the woods. He's nothing to worry about, he keeps himself to himself and anyway, he's completely mad.'

As soon as they resumed their digging, Charlie made a swift retreat. This time, he kept one eye on the men and one eye on the ground in front of him. He wouldn't make the same mistake twice.

Once safely out of sight, he took a deep breath. One thing worried him, though. Had Catweazle been there of his own accord, or had he been following Charlie? The thought gave him the heebie-jeebies, and a shiver ran down his spine. What if he was being watched or followed even now? He picked up the pace, which increased with every step closer to safety. Finally, he came sprinting out of the woods to Lizzie.

'Crikey, what's up with you, seen a ghost or something?'

Charlie, now feeling mildly embarrassed and not wanting to deter Lizzie from her foray into the woods, didn't let on.

'Thought I'd run, then I'd get back here quicker to help you.'

'Thanks,' said Lizzie, not believing a word.

His heart was still racing away, so he had a quick swim and a nice cold drink to calm down.

The routine carried on for the rest of the day with nothing major to report, but Charlie swallowed his pride and told Lizzie about stubbing his toe and the men coming to find him, just so she would take extra care when it was her turn. Although she was incredibly annoying most of the time, he was her elder brother, so tried to look after her.

He never let on how frightened he had been, but the more he mulled things over, the more he sensed Catweazle was there, watching, waiting.

Chapter 9:   Another One!

The next morning, Mrs Baldwin asked Sandra if she could organise a packed lunch for them. It would make a pleasant change and she was looking forward to more tasty Caribbean food.

Over breakfast, Mr Baldwin hit the children with the bombshell that they were going to try a beach on the other side of the island. They had already looked at a map and checked with Burty. The best snorkelling on the island was at Fisherman's Cove, which had a beautiful sandy beach to boot. It was slightly too far to walk with all their gubbins in this heat, so they'd organised a taxi for ten o'clock. It would only take about fifteen minutes by car.

'But we haven't finished exploring the other bay yet,' said Lizzie. 'And aren't you interested in what the Wolfes are doing?'

'Not at all, are you? In fact, that's one reason we thought about moving somewhere else, a little privacy,' said Mr Baldwin.

'But the bay is massive, Dad, and we've only just started checking it out. You never know what we might find.' Charlie thought this might tweak their interest knowing his father's work situation, but his parents were unmoved.

'We're only here for a couple of weeks, so we should make the most of it.'

'But.' Charlie was trying to think of another argument, but his mind fell blank. He felt his stomach twisting, which put him in two minds whether to tell them the truth, but who knew how they would react. No, now wasn't the time.

Mrs Baldwin finished her last mouthful and put down her book.

'Don't forget this isn't just your holiday, it's your father's and mine too.' There was a firmness in her voice that had been missing lately.

Lizzie looked on as she spoke. Annoying as it was, it was nice to be getting her old mum back.

Their father seemed to be extremely excited, but the rest of the family paid no heed to this. He often seemed to live in a world of his own. What they hadn't spotted was that he was being unusually protective of his rucksack, not letting it out of his sight for an instant.

To everyone's surprise, the taxi turned up at ten o'clock on the dot and an exhausted-looking Tallboy greeted them.

'Good morning, people.'

'Good morning, Tallboy,' replied an embarrassed sounding Mr Baldwin. The name Tallboy still sounded strange and rather too familiar.

'So, it's off to Fisherman's Cove. You'll have a great time. Keep your eye out for lobsters if you go snorkelling. There are plenty on that side of the island. Now let me put your bags in the back.'

The children looked at each other. The lobster hunting sounded quite exciting. Perhaps they could even get some for this evening's dinner.

'If we catch a lobster, can we keep it?' asked Lizzie.

'Certainly young lady, just bring it back and I'm sure Burty's chef will prepare something for you.'

With the mention of Burty's chef, Mrs Baldwin suddenly realised they had forgotten the packed lunch. She whipped back through the door to the restaurant where she almost bumped into Sandra walking in the other direction, holding their picnic.

'I heard the taxi arrive and thought you might have forgotten this.'

'Thanks Sandra, I have been rather forgetful lately.'

'No problem at all. Have a great day.'

Mr Baldwin was already sitting in the front seat, holding tight to the rucksack on his knee. With everyone else in the car and their bags packed in the boot, they set off. They had forgotten just how enormous Tallboy was until they were all squeezed into his car. But it wouldn't be for long, or at least that would have been the case had Tallboy driven at a normal speed. So almost twenty minutes and goodness knows how many of his stories later, they pulled up next to a beautiful bay.

'Here we are.'

It was an unbelievable spot. The sand was a beautiful creamy white and the water crystal clear with the occasional patch of colour where the coral was growing beneath. At the far end of the beach, the ground rose vertically, forming a dramatic cliff face, in the middle of which was an enormous cave. Above the cliff stood a small tree-covered hill.

'Welcome to Fisherman's Cove,' said Tallboy, grabbing the bags from the boot. 'And don't forget your picnic.'

Mr Baldwin smiled. 'Thanks again, Tallboy. Would it be ok to get a lift back at four o'clock? We'll stay around here so we won't be difficult to spot.'

'Sure, no problem. See you later,' and he got back into his car and pulled away, slowly.

As it was so picturesque and because of its accessibility, the beach was busier than they would have liked. But it was still a fantastic spot. They walked for 100 yards and found a quiet area to settle down in. The road curved gently away from the beach, so as they put down their towels, all they could hear were the birds and the swooshing of the waves on the beach.

With his mind firmly on the other side of the island, Charlie was on autopilot.

'Let's go snorkelling,' said Lizzie, pushing her brother's mask into his hand.

They wandered down to the sea in silence. It was even more spectacular than they had imagined and proved a pleasant distraction. The coral reefs were close to shore and the abundance of brightly coloured fish made it a truly wonderful spectacle, and for a time, the children's minds were a million miles from Gravedigger's Bay. Charlie pointed down to a hole in the coral and Lizzie saw the rather large and dangerous looking head of an eel, mouth ajar, with needle-like teeth. It monitored every single movement as they swam past. Much to their frustration, the one

72

thing they hadn't spotted were any of the lobsters that Tallboy had mentioned.

Half an hour later, they were back to reality and on their towels. Mrs Baldwin looked at Charlie and Lizzie's red backs, feeling slightly guilty.

'Sun cream please children,' she said, throwing them the bottle. 'And cheer up, we're on a beach in the Caribbean and the sun's shining. What more could you want?'

If you only knew, Charlie thought to himself.

Mr Baldwin decided he needed to go for a quick dip to cool off. Five minutes later and suitably refreshed, he declared he was going off to do a little exploring of his own, and he popped on his shorts and t-shirt, grabbed his rucksack and headed off.

'Where are you going?' said his wife.

'I saw some tracks leading up to the top of the rock face. I thought I'd take some photos of you all from up there.'

Without another word, he headed off in the cave's direction, disappearing into the undergrowth at the edge of the beach. The small hill beyond the cliff was a popular destination judging by the worn track, so he made a minor detour away from the usual thoroughfare. He needed a safe place to conceal something special, but it was proving difficult. Then he spotted a small pile of rocks. He hoped it wasn't anything significant, but needs must, so with another glance around to make sure nobody was watching, he reached into his bag. Time was of the essence, and not thirty seconds later, it lay out of sight beneath the rocks. Feeling rather pleased with himself, he returned to the track and continued his ascent.

Mrs Baldwin stayed with the bags whilst the children went off snorkelling. This time they walked quite a way down the beach before going into the water as they wanted to dive around the bottom of the rock face and explore the cave if the water was deep enough.

A yell from the top of the cliff interrupted the silence. Mrs Baldwin lay down her book and looked up. Her husband was waving, camera in hand. She waved and saw him pointing the camera in her direction. Below him, she could just make out the tops of the children's snorkels as they swam by the cave entrance.

By the time Mr Baldwin returned, his wife was getting rather hot, as was he after his exertions. They shouted to the children and beckoned them back.

'Can you children wait here with the bags while Mum and I go for a swim?'

'Sure,' replied Charlie. 'If you want to go snorkelling, you should go over to the cave. There are loads of fish there.'

'Any lobsters?'

'What do you think?' said Lizzie.

As soon as they got back, Mrs Baldwin announced it was lunchtime. With great excitement, she dug into the cool bag and pulled out two tubs. One contained grilled chicken on wooden skewers in a tangy, fruity sauce, and the other a sweet potato curry flavoured with coconut. To wash that down, there were two large bottles of water. It was simple, different, and absolutely delicious.

Feeling replete, the entire family lay there in the shade, reading their books, and it wasn't long before they had all dozed off.

Mr Baldwin snapped out of his lethargy first. He had thought himself too excited to fall asleep, but it was such a relaxing place and with a full stomach and the calming sound of the waves, it could and probably would have happened to anyone.

'Right everyone, wakey-wakey. Time and tide wait for no man.'

He gave the children a quick nudge each and ran into the sea. As he looked back at the beach, he finally saw movement coming from their direction.

'Come on children, I want to show you something.'

As the children walked towards the sea, Mr Baldwin was walking to meet them.

'Have a quick swim and then we'll be off.'

Following their swim, they went over to join their father, batteries once again fully charged.

'What is it that's so exciting?' said Lizzie.

'Come and see the view from the top of the cliff. You can see clear to the other side of the island. Anyway, the exercise will do you good.'

'I think I'd rather go snorkelling,' said Charlie.

'Go with your father for a change. I'm sure he'd like some company. And you can tell me what's over the hill. It might be of interest for later in the week.'

'Do we really have to?'

'Come on, Lizzie, where's your sense of adventure? Imagine what I used to get up to with my parents when I was your age,' replied her mother.

'I don't have to imagine. You've told us a thousand times already.'

Begrudgingly, the children set off with their father. It was going to be hot, tiring and incredibly boring.

They left the beach and started the gentle climb up the track towards the top of the rock face.

'Why don't we spread out and look for lizards,' said their father. 'I used to love doing it when I was your age.'

This tweaked the children's interest. They hadn't seen many lizards since arriving on the island. The ones they had spotted had been bigger than usual and quite different from those they'd ever seen before. Their favourite was a brown one they kept seeing back at Burty's, with its bulging eyes and extraordinarily long toes.

'Ok,' they replied simultaneously.

'Perfect, I'll go over here to the left and you go over there to the right. Don't forget to look under any rocks if you see them. That's where they often hide.' This wasn't quite true, as lizards normally bask in the sun, but he needed them to find what he'd hidden, so the odd clue wouldn't go amiss.

The time ticked by until finally there was a shout.

Mr Baldwin walked towards them, a little spring in his step. As he got closer, he saw them pointing at an enormous, bright green iguana with a stripy tail and a huge double chin. It was standing there motionless, watching them. It was a wonderful sight, appearing somewhat prehistoric with the barbs along its back. Then, without warning, it turned and scampered off. The children hurried after it, but it had been too quick.

'Perhaps it's gone in here,' Charlie said, pointing at the pile of rocks.

'Make sure you lift the rocks really carefully, just in case it's there. You don't want to hurt it,' said Mr Baldwin. 'And don't forget, there might be scorpions!'

The children had been paying attention, and they tentatively took the pile apart. They were concentrating so much on keeping an eye out for lizards and scorpions that it took some time before Charlie noticed the rolled-up piece of paper. It looked like a piece of old rubbish that had spent too much time in the sun, so he wasn't overly excited as he began unravelling it. As he read it, his jaw dropped in amazement. Standing there in complete silence, he handed it over to Lizzie.

'Well, what is it?' said their father.

'It's a set of instructions,' said Lizzie, almost in a trance, 'to pirates' treasure.'

'Very funny,' said Mr Baldwin, not wanting to give the game away. 'What is it really?'

With that, Lizzie read it out loud:

Be ye tall, short, young or old,
Ye have found the map to pirates' gold.
First seek two stones set by a tree,
Then take three steps towards the sea.
Next, two to the left and two to the right.

Now start digging with all thy might.

'Let's show Mum,' she said, bounding back down the hill.

Chapter 10:   The Deserted Hut

By the time Mr Baldwin arrived back at the towels, the children were in a great state of excitement. But how on earth would they find two stones set by a tree on an island this size? Even though the island wasn't that big, there were an awful lot of trees.

Mr Baldwin looked across at his wife, quite proud of his achievement. Charlie and Lizzie had been obsessed with pirates from an early age, so this time, he had made them a treasure of their own. He had written the clues using an old ink pen, then aged the paper by burning the edges and staining it yellow with old tea bags. The hard part was getting the treasure itself. He'd made countless phonecalls to friends and family asking for any unused costume jewellery. So many people gave a little something. In fact, the box he'd made in his workshop for it all was full in no time. As he had said to the children before, this was going to be the holiday of a lifetime; he would make sure of that.

The children spent the rest of the day discussing what they were going to do now? Should they follow the map, or the clues? They finally settled on the only course of action that Charlie deemed logical. The original map showed something without pinpointing exactly where. It was so vague they were extremely unlikely to find anything, anyway. Even if they did, it might be worthless. As Charlie kept telling Lizzie, the map might just show the location of the graves. The clues were far more specific. OK, it wasn't what they had originally come for, but at last luck was on their side. There was mention of pirates' gold and a precise location. They would need to search well, but it had to be the one to go for. It might take time, but the result would make the effort worthwhile.

Fisherman's Cove was as good a place as any to start, so Charlie and Lizzie spent the rest of the afternoon scouring the edge of the beach for two stones set by a tree. Their search was in vain, but they didn't worry. It was the first place they'd tried. Tomorrow would be another day, and if they had their way, another location.

The next morning at breakfast, to Charlie and Lizzie's delight, their parents asked them where they would like to go. They had already searched Fisherman's Cove, so anywhere else would do.

'How about Gravedigger's Bay again?' said Charlie. If they couldn't find the stones, then at least they could busy themselves with the other treasure.

With everyone agreed, Mrs Baldwin took the unilateral decision to order another picnic from Sandra. Thirty minutes later, they were grabbing their gear and setting off. The children were happier this time. They didn't have to lug their metal rods all the way to the bay. But their buoyant mood didn't last for long, their mother spotting they had hands free and getting them to carry an extra bag each. After a lot of huffing and puffing, they arrived at the beach.

Charlie glanced across at the Wolfes. They wouldn't need binoculars for long. Their men worked relentlessly, and the gap was closing fast.

'We'd better get started, Lizzie,' said Charlie, a sense of urgency in his voice. 'Let's do a bit here first. We can look for the stones later.'

Charlie looked at Lizzie, who stood there pointing, mouth wide open. 'Someone's moved our markers!'

'And I bet I can guess who the SOMEONE is. We'll just have to retrace our steps a little. It shouldn't take long.'

They knew the starting point, so all they needed to do was estimate how far they had gone. To make sure they missed nothing, they retraced their steps a few yards. Although it meant checking a small piece of ground twice, they would miss nothing. Once they'd marked things out again, they set off to the bush to get their rods.

This time, they were fuming. Where were their rods? Charlie looked across to where the Wolfe brothers were doing their digging and could see that he and Lizzie were, as before, being watched like a hawk by the brother sitting in a deck chair.

'It must have been them. He's watching us even as I speak.'

'Well, it's not worth crying over spilt milk. We'll just have to use something else today. Then, with any luck, we can get some more metal rods from the building site when we get back this evening.'

They shouted to their parents, letting them know they were off into the woods.

Consisting almost entirely of coconut palms, the sparsely populated woodland meant finding replacements was proving difficult. But the children persevered, and after a few minutes they noticed a rundown, uninhabited, old shack.

'There must be something there we can use, Charlie.'

It was a ramshackle old building, which was not only in a state of disrepair but, by the look of all the things that had been used to construct it, wouldn't have been much better in its heyday. Old wooden planks formed the walls, these holding up a roof of corrugated iron, rusted through by the salty sea air. A single window provided light, but rather than glass, it had a wooden shutter over it. And next to the window was a door, similar in style to the walls, held closed by a piece of string wound round a nail.

'Let's see inside,' said Lizzie, her curiosity getting the better of her.

Charlie unwound the string and had to lift the door as he pulled it open. The shack was dark inside, with rays of light beaming in through small holes in the structure. There was no floor to speak of, just sand hardened with time. A small wooden bed stood against the right-hand wall. Whoever built the shack had also made the bed looking at the state of it. Some old blankets covered it, a grubby heap of clothes serving as a pillow. Against the left-hand wall stood a table, with a piece of paper on it. Charlie and Lizzie moved a little closer. It was a hand-drawn map of the island. It appeared quite accurate, with large sections of coastline crossed off. They looked at Gravedigger's Bay. It showed both their own and the Wolfes' progress. They looked at each other as if hit by a lightning bolt. The shack wasn't uninhabited at all, and whoever lived here had been back recently. Then they spotted the two metal rods resting upright in the far corner of the room. Suddenly, the hut went dark as something, or rather someone, blocked the light in the doorway.

Terrified, and with only one route of escape, they lunged for the door. The man, not expecting them to be there, jumped out of his skin, dropping the bucket of water he was carrying and the coconuts he had under his arm. As they shot past, he grabbed at them but couldn't get a grip. Only wearing their swimming costumes and covered in suntan lotion, they slipped through his grasp. Outside in the fresh air, they ran for their lives towards the safety of the beach. Too scared to glance back, they continued, listening in terror as the footsteps behind them got closer with every step.

'Dad!' they shouted as they came to the edge of the trees. 'Dad!'

Mr Baldwin, hearing the fear in their voices, jumped up.

'What is it?'

They turned around. Nothing but silence.

'There was a man, and he was chasing us,' said Lizzie. 'We found an old hut in the woods. We didn't think that anyone lived there, so we had a look inside. Then a man turned up. He tried to catch us and then chased us all the way back here.'

'I'm pretty sure it was Catweazle,' said Charlie.

'It sounds like you found him alright. Don't you remember what Burty said? If you leave him alone, he'll leave you alone. I am sure there's no harm done, but give him a wide berth and don't go back there again. You don't want to aggravate him. Anyway, everyone deserves some privacy.'

For once, the children completely agreed.

'We can find some more rods when we get back to Burty's, Lizzie. I'm sure there were more at the building site. Anyway, we should steer well clear of the shack. He looked pretty annoyed.'

'Why don't we search for the two stones set by a tree? That's what we came here for, after all.'

Looking for stones at the bottom of a tree, as they had found out the previous day, was quick work, and it wasn't long before they had searched the entire west hand side of the beach. They didn't find the two stones, but they avoided complete disappointment by coming across two long, thin sticks. They weren't perfect, but sufficient to resume their original search.

The children felt less at ease now than they had ever felt before. On the one hand, they were permanently under the watchful eye of the Wolfes. On the other, Catweazle would be close by, watching, waiting, which was even scarier. The only thing that gave them a little solace was that Catweazle was watching both groups, so fingers crossed he might just as easily be at the other end of the bay checking on how the Wolfes were progressing.

Other than the occasional root, there was little cause for excitement. They had hit something they thought quite promising at one stage, which was larger than the average root, but it just turned out to be an old oil can that had most probably floated ashore and disappeared beneath the sand in the fullness of time. This find ensured they wouldn't get too excited when they hit something the next time, so they expected little when the stick stopped unexpectedly. It wasn't too deep, perhaps 2 feet below the surface, so it didn't take them long to dig the sand out. Charlie was probing with both hands when his right-hand index finger got stuck in something. He wiggled his finger slightly. It moved unhindered, so whatever he had hold of was hollow. He gave it a big tug and to his and Lizzie's horror, he pulled out a skull by its eye socket.

They looked at it, yellow with age, with its two big, almost square eye sockets and a third triangular hole where the nose would have been. The front teeth were missing, both top and bottom. Whoever the owner was would have looked pretty tough in his day. The children sat there, stunned. It doesn't matter what anyone thinks, finding a skull is scarier than you imagine when you actually do it.

'Crikey. What do we do now?' Lizzie said eventually.

'Make sure nobody has seen it for a start, at least until we've decided what to do.'

They put the skull back in the hollow they had made in the sand and ran to get their parents.

'My goodness,' said Mr Baldwin, 'I wonder if you've hit the edge of the graves Burty was telling us about. That'll teach me to doubt what he says in the future.'

Mrs Baldwin picked the skull up discretely and turned it around. It looked in pretty good shape, she thought. No cracks or other signs of a violent end. The teeth looked manky though, few of them and those that were there were more black than white. It brought back happy memories of the stranger holidays she had with her parents when she was a child, and a smile came to her face.

Chapter 11:   Almost Famous

'Hmmm, what on earth should we do with a skull?' said Mr Baldwin, churning things over in his mind.

'As long as nobody else has seen it, I suggest leaving it here,' said Mrs Baldwin.

'Good idea,' said Lizzie, 'I don't fancy sleeping with that in the room.'

'We must mark the exact location, but that'll be easy. We can ask Burty what to do when we get back to town. He might not know himself, but he'll know someone who does.'

Lizzie kept an eye out while Charlie reburied the skull. When he'd finished, he paced out the exact distance to the nearest tree and made a small notch in the trunk with his penknife. Nobody was going to foil them this time.

The Wolfes were watching them like hawks, but everything had happened so fast and they were far enough away that there was only the remotest chance of them seeing anything. More worrying was Catweazle. He must have been keeping a close eye on them to know where they had hidden their rods. Summing up all their courage, Charlie and Lizzie did a quick scout of the woods to see if he was there. The coast was clear.

That was enough excitement for one day, and they'd remained unscathed. Now it was time for a well-earned snorkel.

As soon as they got back to Burty's, Mr and Mrs Baldwin went to find the man himself and tell him about the children's discovery. Burty seemed as surprised as the rest of them. Although he had told the story of Gravedigger's Bay countless times before, exactly as it had once been told to him, he'd never been one hundred percent convinced it was true. He had a real spring in his step as he set off to find the island's only police officer.

Half an hour later, whilst they were enjoying their early evening cocktails, Burty and a smartly dressed young police officer joined them.

'Mr and Mrs Baldwin, meet Blue.'

After the usual pleasantries, Blue asked them the details of their find. Mr Baldwin explained it was, in fact, the children who had made the discovery. Realising it would be easier if the children were present, Mrs Baldwin rose from her chair and nipped off to find them.

The children were hiding the new rods they had purloined from the building site when they heard their mother calling. This time, they rushed back to their room and washed the rust off their hands to stop any needless questioning. Then, they followed their mother back to the bar, where they met Blue.

Blue was young and easy to talk to, and the children answered all his questions without hesitation. It seemed he, too, appreciated that the pirate story might be true. Only possibly at this stage, of course. He was a police officer, so needed to see things for himself and rule out any other possibilities.

Satisfied with everything he had been told, they all agreed to meet the following day after breakfast. Then the children could show Blue the exact location of their find. It had already become rather exciting news, having travelled around the local population like wildfire. Strange for a secret, thought Charlie. Most exciting of all though, the children were going to get their photographs taken for the newspaper. Their photos in the paper; they were almost famous!

The next morning, Mr Baldwin got up just before the sun came over the horizon. He grabbed the spade he had borrowed from Burty the previous evening from the corner of the room. Next, he pulled his suitcase out from under the bed and took out a box, which he popped into his rucksack. After gulping down a glass of water, he opened the door and strode off up the road. He was in a hurry, knowing the children had been waking up early. Everything needed completing and he should be back in his room before there was any sign of life from the room next door.

As he was on his own, it was much quicker than usual, and less than twenty minutes later, he was at the beach in Gravedigger's Bay. Another advantage of the early morning start was that he could avoid the inquisitive eyes of both the Wolfe brothers and Catweazle.

Having had a good scan around for any unwanted visitors, he walked into the trees and retrieved the two stones. He had hidden them the previous day whilst the children were off discovering Catweazle's humble abode. Stones in hand, he continued walking almost to the end of the beach, to be as far away from the Wolfes as possible. After checking again for any undesirable presence, he placed the stones at the base of a palm tree and started pacing. Three, two and then the final two. This is it, he thought to himself. He took the spade and dug down about two feet. Then he plucked the wooden box from his rucksack and dropped it into the hole. Before covering it, he had one last thorough look around to check he wasn't being watched. Finally, he refilled the hole and patted down the sand until it looked as if no one had been there at all.

He set off back to Betty's Guesthouse, feeling rather pleased with himself. As he crept into the room, the sound of his wife gently snoring away welcomed him. He slipped off his shoes, and ever so gently opened the door linking the two rooms. To his great relief, there lay his children, fast asleep. Job done, he thought.

After breakfast, Blue arrived to get the children. Accompanied by their father, they jumped into Blue's rather old, but very cool pickup truck. This was a much more fun way of getting there, they thought to themselves, lurching from side to side as the truck trundled up the track. Five minutes later, they stopped as close as they could to the beach and jumped out.

'Right, if you could give me a hand to carry a few things, I would be extremely grateful.'

He reached into the back of the pickup and handed out a load of wooden stakes. He grabbed a roll of tape and a few other bits and bobs, then asked the children to take him to where they had found the skull. As they walked along, he explained that the first thing he had to do was determine the skull's origins. Was it one of the crew from Burty's story, or was it a body washed ashore at some stage in the past? It could even be the remains of someone murdered years ago on the island, then their body 'disposed of'. You could hear from the tone in his voice that he wanted it to be the last option. It didn't seem like much crime occurred at all on this small island, so this could be Blue's big chance to make a name for himself.

The children found the tree with the notch carved into it, and Charlie started walking towards the sea. After a few paces, he dug his heel into the sand.

'This is it.'

Blue got down on one knee and, rather than using his shovel, began digging with his bare hands. He explained he was doing this to avoid damaging the skull or anything else that was with it. It didn't take long and before you could say Jack Robinson, Blue was holding the skull aloft. It looked rather old, he surmised, judging by the state of the teeth, which were without doubt from a time before dental hygiene had become the norm.

'And you say you have looked over there as well and found nothing,' said Blue, pointing to where the children had originally started their search.

'That's correct,' replied Lizzie.

'We must cordon off this section of the beach then,' he said, pointing to where Charlie and Lizzie were moving onto next.

'Well, that's just great,' said Lizzie under her breath. 'What now?'

'We'll concentrate on the other treasure like we agreed,' whispered Charlie.

Blue got out four stakes and placed them in a large rectangle, from a few yards to the east of the skull, which had already been dug up by the children, to some forty yards to the west. He then asked for everyone's help in putting stakes at four yard intervals around the perimeter. You could see by his face he was finding it hard to contain a smile. But it was serious business, so he tried. When they were all done, he got out a roll of brand new red and white striped tape and wound it around the stakes, sealing off the entire area. Finally, Blue put up the "Police: Keep Out" sign he had carried down with him. He gathered everything and everyone together and they made their way back to the truck.

In all the excitement, they had completely forgotten about the photographer who they found waiting for them back at Burty's. To Mr Baldwin's frustration, the photographer asked for various photographs of the children with Blue holding the skull. It was as if he wasn't even there.

'Fame at last, Lizzie,' said Charlie. He hadn't spotted the rather disappointed expression on his father's face, nor the huge grin on Blue's.

'Which paper will it be in?' Lizzie asked Blue.

'The Gazette, it comes out on Fridays, so a week tomorrow.'

When the photographer had finished, he thanked them all and went on his way. Blue expressed his gratitude to Mr Baldwin and the children for their help and said he would contact them if he had any further questions. With that, Mrs Baldwin joined the rest of the family and they sauntered off towards their rooms.

'That'll be so cool. I can't wait until next Friday,' said Lizzie.

'It's rather annoying that they've fenced off where we were digging. Why couldn't the Wolfes have found the skull? It just isn't fair,' said Charlie.

Mr Baldwin then chirped up that he was certain everything would turn out ok and anyhow, it was one heck of a holiday so far. They had found a treasure map and a human skull. Few people back home would believe that.

'But one thing's been puzzling me. I know it's probably just a coincidence the Wolfes being here, but what on earth are they doing with those two men in Gravedigger's Bay? Do you think they have just heard the same story as us and are trying their luck at finding something? They look terribly out of place on the beach.'

'They both look so creepy. Perhaps looking for skeletons is something they do every holiday,' said Mrs Baldwin with a smile. 'Now, let's get our thinking caps on. Where shall we go today?'

'Let's go somewhere new. The usual bay's going to be like Piccadilly Circus.'

This was exactly what the children wanted to hear. A brand new location to search for the two stones set by a tree. As for the digging, it was impossible for them to continue for the time being. But they were there for another eight days, so there was still plenty of time.

With their bags packed, they sat at the table outside their rooms and looked at the map.

'How about Gull Point?' suggested Mr Baldwin. 'Not much of a sandy beach, by the look of it, but plenty of rocks for snorkelling.'

'Can we find a slightly more sheltered beach?' asked Lizzie. 'Preferably with some trees, then we can explore and go snorkelling. What about here, Yeaman's Bay?' she continued, tapping the map.

Mrs Baldwin appreciated some shade, and with everyone in agreement, they set off for Yeaman's Bay. It was further than their usual destination but took almost the same time to get there as most of the walking was along the road. It was only the last few hundred yards where they had to make their way through a thinly wooded area of palm trees to the beach. Once again, they found themselves treated to a beautiful expanse of white sand, with only two other families around to disturb them. They found the perfect spot and settled in the shade of a large palm tree overhanging the beach.

As picturesque as it was, Mr Baldwin and the children were soon getting increasingly bored. The beach was OK, the snorkelling too, but once Charlie and Lizzie had checked under every tree for two stones, it wasn't long before they had had enough.

'Right, who thinks it would be fun to see what Blue's up to?' asked Mr Baldwin.

'Can we, please?' Lizzie begged her mother.

Mrs Baldwin capitulated more easily than they had expected. She was enjoying her book and thought a short trudge round to their usual bay would be much easier to take than an entire afternoon of moaning. At least then she could read in peace.

'OK. Let's have lunch when we get there. It's going to be quite a trek from here, at least forty minutes, I would guess.'

She was right, and forty-five minutes later, they walked onto the beach at Gravedigger's Bay.

It was a lot busier than any of them imagined it was going to be. Blue was there with four other people. Two men and a woman were carefully digging around a now headless skeleton using hand-held tools. Another man photographed it all from every imaginable angle. Meanwhile, Blue seemed to be furiously taking notes.

'These are the children who found the skull,' he announced when he saw Charlie and Lizzie.

'Pleased to meet you,' said the lady. 'We're here to find out who this might be and what happened to him.'

'I bet it's a pirate,' said Lizzie.

'It might well be. We'll just have to wait and see.'

After a brief conversation, they said their goodbyes and continued along the beach.

'Let's try to get some privacy,' said Mr Baldwin, walking almost to the end. 'Here, this'll do.'

He set down his bags and the rest of the family followed suit, putting their towels down and readying for today's picnic.

Mrs Baldwin was already licking her lips in anticipation of the delights prepared for them today. She got out the tubs and couldn't help notice the disappointment on the children's faces. There seemed to be rather a lot of salad. Thankfully, one contained pieces of chicken, so she wouldn't have to put up with too much moaning.

After lunch, with one parent napping and the other enjoying their book, the children took a walk up the beach to see what was going on. They were not only keen to see what else Blue's team had uncovered, but also to get closer to the Wolfes, who were themselves taking an active interest in the goings on in the middle of the bay.

As Charlie and Lizzie got closer to the taped off area, they noticed Catweazle crouching amongst the trees. Busy watching the digging going on, he was blissfully unaware of their presence. Because of this, it gave them ample time to give him a proper once over. He was tall and thin, as they already knew, but he looked very healthy. Because of his long hair and beard, he looked quite old, but his body told a different story, and the children surmised he couldn't be much older than their father. He must have sensed that he was being watched as suddenly he turned, made eye contact with the children, and in an instant disappeared into the undergrowth.

Chapter 12:   Two of Them

Although not much time had passed, the excavation team had made rapid progress. Not three feet from the first skeleton, the team worked away furiously. As the children approached, they spotted another skull in the sand and a larger skeleton being uncovered.

'Another one!' said Charlie to his sister.

The lady to whom he had spoken before heard him and lifted her head.

'It's my betting that we'll find more bodies, and it's the burial site alluded to in all the stories of old. The two bodies are lying in exactly the same direction, which means it's unlikely that they were just washed ashore. Blue has checked the police records and nobody on the island had gone missing in years.'

'It's exciting though,' said Lizzie, 'I just hope it doesn't mean that loads of people will come here all the time; it's so peaceful.'

'Well, if that's the case, so be it. At least the island will benefit from the tourism.'

'Depends how you think of it, I suppose,' said Charlie. He, like Lizzie, rather enjoyed having an island pretty much to themselves.

They carried on down the beach towards the Wolfes, emboldened by having Blue close by, although they lacked the courage to get too close. The men were still busy with the digging and filling of holes. As usual, the children were being watched like hawks through the binoculars. Nothing seemed to have changed, so they concluded that whatever the Wolfes were after, which was undoubtedly the same as them, they hadn't found it either.

With an immense sense of relief, the children turned and headed back to their parents.

'We should really walk along the treeline,' said Charlie. 'Don't forget, we're still looking for the two stones.'

'But we've already checked here.'

'It always pays to keep an eye out, just in case we've missed anything.'

Once they had passed by the excavation site again, which appeared to have grown yet again in the minutes since they were there, they wandered to the edge of the beach.

'I wonder what our photo is going to be like in the paper,' said Lizzie.

'And what they say about us. I tell you what though, I can't wait to show everyone when we get back home. They wouldn't believe any of this without proof.'

As they sauntered along, chatting to one another, Lizzie suddenly stopped in her tracks. They were now only about ten yards from their parents, but clear as day, there they were, two stones at the base of a palm tree. She looked at Charlie, who looked back at her, then as one, they ran back as fast as humanly possible to their parents.

'Can't talk now,' said Charlie, grabbing the foldable spade from his bag. They'd repeated the rhyme to themselves time and again and knew the words by heart. But they needed to get this right, so when they got to the tree, they both took a deep breath. Mr Baldwin was watching them with a huge grin on his face, then he could resist no longer. He got up and walked towards the children, camera in hand. Meanwhile, Lizzie started the pacing.

Three steps towards the sea, then turn left, two more paces, now turn right and two more paces. Lizzie marked an 'X' in the sand with her toes.

'Here!'

Charlie thrust the spade into the sand and started digging frantically.

Nothing at first, but he persevered, still nothing.

'Keep going,' said their father, encouraging him on.

There was a clunk, the sound of metal on metal. Charlie had hit something. He and Lizzie stopped for a minute to check they weren't being watched. They glanced back to the Wolfes and the excavation site, then to the treeline. Confident that they were alone, they continued digging with their hands. Their eyes grew wider as they uncovered the booty, bit by bit. As they brushed the sand away from the wood, they saw it, an oak chest, a treasure chest.

Mr Baldwin looked on, confused.

'No, no, that's not it, no!'

He strode back to the tree and paced out three, then two, then two. Because of his longer stride, he was at least two feet from where the children were crouching on the ground. He started digging like a man possessed, while his astonished children looked on.

'Here it is, here!' he said, pulling a black box from the sand.

The children looked on, confused.

'I, I found it earlier,' he stuttered, realising he was about to receive a barrage of questions.

'Why didn't you say something?' said Lizzie in a somewhat disbelieving voice.

'We can talk about that later.' Charlie was getting impatient. 'Let's get this one out first.'

As hard as they tried, the children couldn't shift the chest. It was enormously heavy.

'Let me try,' said their father, easing in between them.

No matter how much he tugged, Mr Baldwin couldn't shift it either. It's not attached to anything, he thought, but to make sure he rummaged around in the sand underneath the chest. Nope, nothing there.

'It's locked anyway, so if it's too heavy to shift, perhaps we should cover it up again,' said Charlie. 'We can have a good think about what to do and come back tomorrow. In the meantime, we can have a look at the one Dad "found earlier".'

'Are you mad?' said Lizzie, facing her brother. 'We've just found treasure and you want to leave it here on the beach!'

Mr Baldwin, seeing what was about to start, stepped in.

'We have to be practical here, Lizzie. Nobody was watching you, so it should be safe for one more day. Anyway, the excavation will keep most people away from the beach. They'll want to find somewhere more tranquil.'

'Somewhere without skeletons,' said Charlie, trying to make light of things. He had butterflies in his stomach. He knew the importance of today's finds more than anyone. There was no way he was going to lose anything now, not after all the effort they'd gone to.

As quickly as they could, the children covered over the wooden chest with sand and flattened the entire area. They turned their attention to the black box and noticed it had a rather rudimentary skull and crossbones drawn on it and a simple clasp with no lock. This one wouldn't be a problem to open. In a great state of excitement, the children took the box back to where their mother was sitting, still oblivious to everything, reading her book.

'Look, Mum,' said Charlie.

Mrs Baldwin looked up. 'Wow, have you checked if there's anything in it?'

'Not yet!' said Lizzie, finding it difficult to contain herself.

They all sat round in a circle with the box on the ground between them. The children, in their elation, forgot to check for any onlookers and opened the box. Their eyes almost came out on stalks and their jaws dropped, for what confronted them was the box full to the brim with various types of jewellery. Rings, earrings, necklaces, brooches, you name it, and it was there. Everywhere they looked, they seemed to see more; diamonds, rubies, sapphires, everything imaginable.

Mr Baldwin had been ready with his camera when the children opened the box. Their faces were a picture, mouths wide open, although the genuine excitement was difficult to capture on film. Not a minute later, there they sat, bedecked with every type of jewellery available. They couldn't wait to see the Wolfe brothers' expressions as they paraded the pirate treasure in front of them later that evening.

Having been busy with the camera and taken some nice shots for posterity, Mr Baldwin's mind wandered. He was thinking of the chest. It seemed to have appeared from nowhere. Unlike the treasure consisting entirely of costume jewellery he had put together with the rest of the family, the treasure chest was nothing to do with him and whatever it contained weighed a ton. But for the time being, there was little chance of it being found. It had been there for goodness knows how long, so it was unlikely that it was going to disappear overnight. Anyway, it was so heavy there was little they could do for the time being, even if they wanted to.

After an afternoon of splashing around in the sea and snorkelling, the children were quite happy when their mother told them it was time to go. They were keen to get back and tell Burty and Sandra the news of their treasure find, which made it all the more frustrating when their parents stopped to talk to Blue and see how he was progressing. It turned out that they had now uncovered a third body, and it looked like there were going to be many more if the old story was anything to go by. If this was the case, Blue said that he might have to ask for a temporary closure of the entire beach until they knew how big the site might be.

Any trace of excitement instantly disappeared from Charlie's face. Closing the beach! Was that really necessary? And now of all times. He looked over at his father. His expression said everything. He was thinking the same.

Then Blue noticed the children, now sporting all manner of trinket.

'What's all that?'

'We dug up some treasure,' said Lizzie, showing Blue the box with the skull and crossbones.

'Lucky you,' said Blue, a smile coming across his face.

'We'd better head off now. We'll probably see you tomorrow,' said Mr Baldwin, his mind elsewhere.

Charlie put all thoughts of the other treasure behind him for the time being. They had one treasure, and if the worst came to the worst, that would have to do. He and Lizzie chatted the entire way home about what they could do with their newfound wealth. They were still talking half an hour later when they walked through the door at Burty's. It had been an exciting but tiring day, so after a quick shower, the children lay down on their beds and within no time at all, they were both fast asleep.

Two hours later, their mother woke them up. It was time to get ready for dinner. They had some celebrating to do, she said, what with the treasure and all, so the children could have whatever they wanted.

As they sat down at the table, Burty came over to ask them what they would like to drink. He looked at the children inquisitively, as they had taken the opportunity not only to dress for dinner but also to wear a large majority of what they had found in the box. They sat there beaming, with their large gaudy necklaces and big gold earrings. They looked like pirates of old, very successful pirates of old at that!

'What on earth is all this?'

Charlie regaled him with the complete account, omitting the fact that they had also happened upon the other treasure chest, of course. Hopefully that would be their job for tomorrow.

Burty was all ears, in particular when they spoke about the progress Blue was making and that the story of Gravedigger's Bay probably was true. Mr Baldwin watched the expression on Burty's face change. He could almost see the dollar signs appearing in his eyes as the children spoke. He was sure Burty had a lot more questions, but those were probably best aimed at Blue, so after the story, Burty took their orders and carried on.

Charlie and Lizzie took their mother up on her offer and ordered steak and chips. The food was as delicious as ever, so didn't take long to finish. It was still early and as the children had already had a nap, their parents suggested a visit to The Grand for an after-dinner drink. They still hadn't talked about the rather important agenda for tomorrow.

As they walked through the door to the hotel, they almost bumped into the Wolfe brothers walking the other way.

'Good evening, and how was your day?' said Edward (or was it Peregrine) Wolfe, admiring the jewellery clad children.

'Good evening,' said Mr Baldwin, 'excellent thanks. Charlie and Lizzie found a box of treasure on the beach. They used a set of clues they discovered on the other side of the island. We're having quite a holiday.'

The Wolfes smiled. They had dealt with a lot of jewellery at auction, so they were quite aware of costume jewellery when they saw it.

'And you, have you been up to anything exciting?' Mr Baldwin had been dying to ask this question for ages. The brothers had spent every day in the bay since they had been here, working their way methodically across toward the skeletons. Whatever they were looking for, it wasn't the graveyard. If that had been the case, they would have given up as soon as they had seen Blue and his team arrive.

'Not much really, just looking for rare shells. People find them in Whaler's Bay on the odd occasion. We've had a couple of local chaps helping us so we can enjoy a relaxing holiday whilst they do the donkey work.'

What a load of old tosh, everyone thought. One thing was for sure, you don't engage the services of two people for the entirety of your holiday just to find "rare shells".

105

'Well, all the best with that. Enjoy the rest of your evening,' said Mr Baldwin as they turned and went their separate ways, but not before the Wolfes had one last look at the children and met their eyes with icy stares.

Chapter 13: Under Cover of Darkness

The Baldwins sat down at a table on the terrace and ordered their drinks, two rum punches and two lemonades. Once these had arrived, the discussion began about what they were going to do the following day. It turned out that Mr Baldwin had told his wife the entire story of the two treasures whilst the children enjoyed their afternoon naps back in their room. This was good news on two counts. It saved a lot of time and, more importantly, it would be better not to discuss such things in public. You never know who might be listening.

There were only two options. Should they try to move the chest in its entirety, or should they force it open and move the chest and its contents bit by bit? It weighed a ton, so moving it in one go had its problems. But so did opening a sturdy-looking lock on the beach with the limited tools at their disposal. The crucial question was how could they execute either plan without drawing attention to themselves? They had to remember that the Wolfes were watching their every move.

'So let's have a vote on it,' said Mr Baldwin. 'Everyone for option 1, raise your hand.'

'Well, that saves any argument,' said Mrs Baldwin, looking at all four arms in the air.

Given how much the chest weighed, Mr Baldwin came up with the idea of shifting it using a sturdy wooden pole and some rope. They would put the rope round the chest and then tie it to the pole. If they took a long enough pole, all four of them could do the lifting if it proved too heavy for two. They would have to think hard about when to do it. Absolute secrecy was crucial. They also needed to get a pole and some rope, leaving them plenty of time to fine tune their plans.

'At least we already have one treasure,' said Lizzie.

'Which reminds me, Dad. How did you know it was there? You never even mention it. It's like it doesn't exist,' said Charlie.

Mr Baldwin shifted uneasily in his chair, then, after what seemed like an age, broke his silence.

'What's better than finding treasure?'

'I don't know. What is better than finding treasure?' answered Lizzie.

'Finding two treasures. We have one. Now let's concentrate on retrieving the other.'

Charlie could see that his father was being evasive, but he was right about concentrating on the one they didn't have, so for the time being he stopped his questioning. He'd try again once they had the chest safely in their possession.

Bright and early the next morning, they finalised their plans over breakfast. For optimum secrecy, they would get the operation underway in the early evening, just after sundown.

After breakfast, the children, accompanied by their father, began their hunt for the pole and rope. This might have proved difficult in some environments, but one thing you find rather a lot of when you are in

108

proximity to the sea and boats are ropes and posts. Whether they were already in use was another question.

Mrs Baldwin decided they needed a change of lunch menu, so headed off to Eglit's Emporium. Whilst there, she noticed several shopping trolleys by the side of the shop. This could be exactly what they needed for the last part of the journey, to get the chest through the town unnoticed. Once she had finished the shopping, she spoke to Vin.

'Can I borrow a trolley to take the shopping back to Burty's?'

'Of course you can, madam. They're always there, people borrow them the whole time and I tell them that as long as they bring them back, they are most welcome to use them. Anyway, it's hard to lose them in a town this size.'

'Thank you. I'll bring it back in a few minutes.' She returned home with the shopping and then popped the trolley back to Eglit's. Perfect, she thought.

Meanwhile, the other three were looking round, particularly amongst the abandoned boats just off the beach, for old bits of rope and a post. They saw lots of rope, some ancient, but inevitably it was already in use. Finally, Mr Baldwin figured out it was time to bite the bullet. They'd passed a boatyard earlier. There had to be something there.

One of the local fishermen was in the yard, busy repainting the hull of his boat.

'Excuse me, but you don't know where we could get some rope and a post?'

109

'If you go into the office and speak to Sharky, he might be able to help,' said the man, pointing to something more akin to a shed that had survived innumerable hurricanes. Inside, there was a man listening to reggae on the radio.

'How can I help you, my friends?'

'We were wondering whether we could borrow or hire a couple of lengths of strong rope and a pole or post.'

'Let's have a look to see what we have,' he said, exiting the office and threading his way through the boats. 'How long do you want it for?'

'Just a few days should do. We're staying up the road at Burty's place.'

'Ah, you know Burty, well then just give me a deposit of $20 and I'll return it when you bring the stuff back. There's no hurry.'

Sharky untied a couple of mooring lines from one of the smaller fishing boats and continued on to a pile of posts.

'One of these will do. They're mooring posts,' he said, 'and don't go worrying yourselves about the rope, the fishing boat's mine.'

'Thank you so much, we'll be back in the next few days,' said Mr Baldwin, reaching into his wallet for a $20 dollar note.

They set off back to the guesthouse, rope and post in hand. Perhaps the post was bigger than would have been ideal, but on the bright side, no matter how heavy the chest was, the post wouldn't break.

Once back at Burty's, they reconvened, checking that they had everything they needed to retrieve the chest. Things were coming together rather nicely, but at this very moment in time, there was nothing they could do. It was broad daylight, and the excavation was in full swing, so all they could do was wait. At dusk and with a deserted beach, they would make their move.

Picnic and rucksacks at the ready, The Baldwin family set off for another day of adventure.

'How about a boat trip?' suggested Charlie.

'If I try to read on a boat I'll only get seasick,' replied his mother.

Blasted books, thought Charlie. How many had she brought, anyway? Their mother always complained about getting seasick, but had they ever seen any evidence of it? Nope.

Mr Baldwin was already striding off, map in hand. There was another bay directly south of the airport that seemed ideal. It looked suitably secluded, only accessible via a small path. It would give them some uninterrupted relaxation time. The children thought it was perfect; they wanted some privacy. They had a lot on their minds and loads to discuss.

The trouble when you are enjoying yourself is that time seems to pass all too quickly, and it didn't seem long before they were packing their bags in readiness for the short walk home. They had spent a small amount of time discussing the evening's plans when they first got there, but there wasn't much to talk about other than what exactly they needed to take.

They didn't want to have to undertake the journey in the semi-darkness more than once.

Back at the guesthouse, they checked and then double-checked everything they needed for their excursion. With the clock passing six and the light fading, they slipped out into the early evening.

The children often took their rucksacks around with them, so it was easy to carry the rope unnoticed. Concealing an enormous post was a different matter. Anyway, all would be fine once they were on the track as nobody travelled to and from the bay after sundown. With their father carrying the post on his shoulder, Charlie and Lizzie thought it great fun telling him people were coming and making him rush for cover. His run was even funnier than normal, and the look on his face was priceless.

'Don't you know about the boy who cried wolf,' said Mr Baldwin? He smiled as he suddenly thought of the Wolfe brothers and realised that he had almost made a joke. Well, he thought it was funny, anyway.

The children stopped mucking around. One warning from their father was enough. They wondered why on earth their mother was there? She wouldn't be doing any of the digging or carrying, and they were already doing the lookout jobs. Then, without warning, Mrs Baldwin crossed the road to Eglit's Emporium and grabbed a trolley.

'It's ok, I've already asked. All we have to do is make sure we bring it back when we've finished. It will make our lives a lot easier once we're back on proper roads and should make the chest less obvious as we come back through the town.'

She rejoined the rest of the team and they carried on up the road to the track. The small trolley wheels were useless on rough ground, so as soon as she found a suitable hiding place, she pushed the trolley off the edge of the track and out of sight, making a large scrape mark with her foot so they'd be sure to find it on the way back.

The light from the town faded into the distance until only the moon guided their way. Charlie felt his trouser pocket. The torch was there, safe and sound. They walked in silence, listening for anything that might spell danger, with only the cicadas for company. The occasional sound of movement in the woods halted them momentarily, but there was sure to be wildlife about and they continued on.

As the track neared the beach, the children put on their torches, making sure not to point them in anyone's face. This wasn't the time you wanted anyone to suffer from night blindness. Everyone needed to have their senses and wits about them. Mr Baldwin stopped and held up his hand.

'Did anyone hear that?' he whispered.

Everyone shook their head. They carried on; senses heightened.

'Shhh,' said Charlie in a hushed voice, 'I heard it, too. I think something or someone's following us.'

'I can't imagine it's a something, more likely a someone,' replied his father.

The children shone their torches at the surrounding trees. Nothing.

As they approached the beach, they noticed that the prohibited area had now doubled in size.

'Let's have a quick look at their progress,' said Mrs Baldwin, heading off towards the children's first discovery. The others followed. They hadn't gone far before an astonishing sight met their eyes. Blue's team had uncovered some fifteen skeletons, each one lying exactly where they had found it. It made for pretty unpleasant night-time viewing and as a gust of wind came across the bay, shivers went down their spines.

'Come on,' said Mr Baldwin, 'we don't want to hang around here too long. Let's get this done and have some dinner.'

They moved back to the west end of the beach, torches shining at the bases of the palms.

'Here we are,' said Lizzie excitedly.

They paced away from the tree toward the sea and started digging. They found nothing at their first attempt, so they went back to the tree and paced it out again. This time they dug ever so slightly to the left of their first spot, and you could see the relief on everyone's faces as the spade clunked against the chest. With Lizzie and her mother keeping a lookout, the other two started digging. It didn't take long, but it got rather frustrating, with the fine sand constantly falling back into the hole from all sides. Finally, with the chest uncovered, they burrowed beneath it and slipped the ropes through. Lizzie was a dinghy sailor, so they left the knots to her and she assured everyone that bowlines would be perfect for the job.

With Charlie at one end of the post and his father at the other, they put it on their shoulders and tried to lift the chest out of the hole. Charlie was struggling and was soon joined by his mother. Slowly, they lifted the chest and put it down on the beach. It was even heavier than they had imagined and was going to take a little longer than they thought to get back to the guesthouse.

'Right,' said Mr Baldwin, 'one, two, three, lift.'

They turned and started the trek back through the woods. The night was still, amplifying the gentle lapping of waves on the beach. As they walked and the sound of the sea receded, so the laboured breathing of the pole bearers took its place. To their left, half a dozen birds took flight. They stopped. As the silence returned, they continued their journey. Another flock of birds screeched their annoyance at being disturbed. Something was there, and it was following them. The weight of the chest made a quick escape impossible, so they stood listening, watching. Lizzie shuddered as she shone her torch towards the sound. Nothing. They carried on until Mr Baldwin held up his hand to signal for them to stop. Voices, and they were getting closer.

Chapter 14:   Who's There?

With their torches off and no night vision to speak of, everything descended into an inky blackness. They had to move fast, so feeling the way with their toes, they retreated away from the track. Even with his mother's help, Charlie's head pounded with the exertion. He thought it was about to explode and was struggling to control his breathing. At last, Mr Baldwin signalled and, as one, they crouched down and waited. The voices grew louder and a ray of light swept over their heads before arcing back in the opposite direction. A bush rustled, and the voices stopped.

'Who's there? This is the police.' It was Blue with one of his team. They must have been going to check on the excavation site.

They scanned the trees again. A sudden shout broke the silence as the torch fixed upon Catweazle, half-hidden behind a tree. With a terrifying screech, he jumped up and ran.

'I should have guessed, Catweazle. Come on, let's carry on.'

The two men disappeared into the distance.

The situation proved frustrating for the Baldwins. With such a heavy cargo they were moving at a snail's pace, so they couldn't carry on for the time being, Blue would head back the same way any moment. They would just have to wait where they were until he had gone.

It didn't take long before Blue and his colleague reappeared, still chatting away. A couple of minutes later, the Baldwins heard the engine roar into life and the truck pulled away. They got to their feet and continued their journey.

Each step was more painful than the last, the pole carving a deep furrow into their shoulders. Stops became more frequent, but they soon forgot the momentary respite, as the colossal weight pressed back down on their bruised bodies. Welcome relief came thirty minutes later when the sound of Blue's truck forced them to seek refuge by the side of the track. Fifteen minutes later, he drove back past. In the semi-darkness, nobody spotted the grimace on Charlie's face as he mustered all his strength and took up the strain.

Finally, they got to the road, but not before Mrs Baldwin had retrieved the shopping trolley from behind the bush. She rejoined Charlie at his end of the pole and, with great care, they lowered the chest into the trolley. Because of the enormous weight, nobody knew whether the wheels were going to work, and there was an audible sigh of relief from Charlie when they did.

Mrs Baldwin reached into her bag and grabbed a couple of towels that she threw over the chest. 'Now, that looks better.'

They met a few people en route and, to their astonishment, not one of them showed any interest in what was in the trolley. It was as Vin had said. People used the trolleys all the time and as long as they returned them, there wasn't an issue.

It was almost half-past eight by the time they had dropped the chest in their room and returned the trolley. They were all very thirsty and absolutely ravenous, so knowing that the restaurant wouldn't be open much longer, they ate before doing anything else.

Exhausted by the day's exertions, dinner was a silent affair. The only thing they wanted to talk about was the chest, which is the one thing they couldn't do, not in public anyway.

Once back in their rooms, the entire family stood around the chest while Mr Baldwin gave it a thorough examination. The whole thing was in fantastic condition given it had been buried for goodness knows how long. Constructed of oak, three metal straps ran from front to back with a further two running across the sides. It was along the central strap over the top and front that their obstacle sat, a rather large metal lock which, although old and weatherworn, remained remarkably shut.

Mr Baldwin had noticed the spade in the corner of the room. He grabbed it and tried prising the lock open, but to no avail. He wished he was back at home. There were so many tools in his workshop that could have done the job, not least an angle grinder which would have sliced through the metal in seconds. But they weren't at home, so they needed to find a different solution.

Charlie got out his Swiss Army knife next and started some futile digging at the lock with most of the tools at his disposal.

Meanwhile, Mrs Baldwin walked to the wardrobe and took out an old metal coat hanger. She bent the last half inch of the metal at right angles by shutting the end in a drawer and pushing down on the rest of the hanger as hard as she could. This done, she handed it to Lizzie, who, insisting it was now her turn to have a go, barged her brother out of the way. With all eyes watching, she started turning the end around in the lock. It was one of those situations where not everyone thought it was the best idea, but hey ho, let her have a go. You can imagine their surprise when there was a sudden click, and the catch moved, albeit a fraction.

'Every problem is a solution in disguise,' said Mrs Baldwin contentedly under her breath.

'Charlie, try to get your blade under the catch and prise it open,' said Lizzie.

Charlie scraped and scratched around the edge of the catch until finally he got the blade underneath. With a bit of twisting, slowly but surely it moved, until hey presto, it flicked open.

There was some hesitation on all sides in lifting the lid, not because they didn't want to, but more to do with the fact that until now, the contents had been solely in their imaginations, and the reality was about to hit.

'Well children,' said their father, 'you found it, so I think you should have the honour of opening it.'

Charlie and Lizzie looked at each other and put their hands on the lid. What they thought would be a relatively easy manoeuvre didn't go according to plan, and the lid remained firmly shut.

'The wood's probably swollen or warped over time,' said Mr Baldwin. 'It'll probably need a massive tug. Use some "elbow grease" as your grandfather used to say.'

The children moved to the back of the chest and, leaning over, grabbed the front top corners and gave an almighty heave. Suddenly, they flew backwards as the lid opened. From their now seated positions on the floor, they still saw the contents and what met their eyes was staggering. They had talked about it being full of jewels and gold, just like they had always seen in films, but that was wishful thinking. What they saw was beyond their wildest dreams. The box was full to the brim with gold coins.

For a moment, nobody said a word, then Mr Baldwin reached forward and plucked out a single coin. It looked like gold and was heavy enough to be gold, but it was strange. It wasn't really circular, as you would have expected it to be. As he looked at the others, he noticed the same. In fact, the only thing which marked them out as coins was the embossing on either side. He passed it to his wife.

Charlie and Lizzie picked a coin out each and looked at them, mesmerised.

'They look like doubloons; do you remember them from our pirate book, Charlie?'

'You're right. That means they really are gold, solid gold.' They'd done it! There was no reason to move house now. A look of sheer joy shot across Charlie's face.

The magnitude of the discovery had quite taken them aback, and it was only after a couple of minutes that they resumed their conversation.

'So, what do we do now?' Mrs Baldwin asked her husband.

'We must hide it, I suppose, at least while we work out a plan of action. The funny thing is, I would have felt a lot more comfortable if it was back where the children found it.'

'I am not taking it back again. I don't think I could carry it another inch,' said Charlie.

'Why not empty some coins out first?' said Lizzie.

They all agreed that it wasn't such a bad idea, so emptied a few handfuls into each of their suitcases and slid them back under the beds. Mr and Mrs Baldwin lifted the chest, which was still unbelievably heavy, into the bottom of the wardrobe. It gave a tremendous sigh under the strain, but held firm. Once safely in situ, Mrs Baldwin covered the chest with the dirty washing.

'Right,' said Mr Baldwin, 'I know there's a lot to talk about, but it's been a long day. Let's have a good night's rest and discuss things in the morning. And don't forget to shut your window, children. There's going to be a storm tonight.'

With everyone in agreement, the children said goodnight and went through the adjoining door to their room, and it wasn't long before they were both fast asleep.

Halfway through the night, something brought Charlie back to the land of the living. Eyes half-open and in a state of semi-consciousness, he watched the curtains dance back and forth in the moonlight. The storm must be over. But something was wrong. The curtains. He thought back to the previous evening. Door, check. Window, check. Charlie scanned the room, keeping his breathing as steady as possible. Then he spotted a near imperceptible movement by the wardrobe. Someone was there. Lizzie? Charlie rolled over. She was facing him, sound asleep. Everything was silent except the metronomic thumping in his head. He rolled again. There it was, the outline of a man, motionless, watching, waiting.

Charlie lay there, unable to move, a thousand and one thoughts going through his head. Everything kept coming back to one question: who would make the first move? He couldn't lie there and wait for fate to take its course. He had to do something. Gathering all his courage, he readied himself. One more second. He leapt from his bed, running as fast as he could to the adjoining door.

'Dad, quick, there's someone in our room.'

Chapter 15:   A Big Mistake

Mr Baldwin was wide awake in an instant. Heart pounding and senses heightened, he leapt out of bed and sprinted to the adjoining door. The intruder made a dash for it, but tripped and crashed to the floor. The commotion woke Lizzie, who sat bolt upright in her bed and started screaming. Frantic scrambling followed as the interloper kicked the web of clothes aside and got to his feet. Mr Baldwin charged in and saw the silhouette of a man by the window. Then, in a flash, he jumped back through and made a dash for it.

Mr Baldwin opened the door and looked out to see Catweazle running into the distance. It would have been futile giving chase, Catweazle would have known the area like the back of his hand after all these years, making escape a foregone conclusion. Mr Baldwin turned, locking the door behind him, then shutting the window.

'Sorry Dad,' said Lizzie, 'it was my fault. The storm had finished, and I was hot, so I opened the window.'

'Don't worry, but it looks like we must all remain extra careful from now on. Let's all go back to bed and get some sleep.'

He checked all the windows and doors before retiring to his bed, where he lay, thinking. Not only was there something in their rooms that most people would love to get their hands on if they knew it was there, but someone did already know! It made him uncomfortable knowing that Catweazle had probably been watching them all evening.

By the morning, and after very little sleep, Mr Baldwin had come up with a plan. Now that they were under the watchful eye of Catweazle, it would be a good idea to move some gold for safekeeping. He suggested bagging up the coins they had put in their suitcases and hiding them in various locations around the island. If they split into two groups to do this, then there was no way that Catweazle could monitor them both. That way, most of the treasure would remain in the safety of their rooms, but it also meant that if something unexpected happened, they wouldn't lose it in its entirety.

With everyone in agreement, time was of the essence. It was far too risky to leave the gold where it was whilst they sauntered off to the beach.

After another splendid but hurriedly eaten breakfast, Mrs Baldwin nipped off to Eglit's Emporium in search of bags. She had a hunt around but couldn't find anything suitable, but just as she was walking out of the door, she spotted potatoes in a thick hessian sack.

'Have you got any spare sacks?' she asked, pointing at the potatoes.

'I'll check out the back. I'm pretty sure we have.' Vin returned with a rather grubby old sack in his hands. 'I've only got the one. Will that do?'

'That's grand. And I'll need some strong fishing line and a needle with an eye big enough to fit it through if possible.'

'Of course, Madam,' he said with a single nod of the head, reaching under the counter for the needle. He then walked to the opposite wall where Mrs Baldwin now noticed all the fishing tackle. 'There'll be no charge for the sack.'

With her mission accomplished, she thanked Vin for his help and headed back to the guesthouse.

Once there, she sat outside with a penknife borrowed from the children, the hessian sack, needle and fishing line and started making the small bags. She finished them rather neatly with a draw-string at the top. They were strong, so they should be to hold the gold coins without breaking.

'That should do it,' she said, sitting back and admiring her work.

With the bags finished, they retrieved the coins from their suitcases and split them into four equal piles. They then bagged them up and put one in each of their rucksacks. Each pair would require a map of the island so they could mark the exact location of each bag, so Charlie popped across to reception and got two new maps from the rack.

Choosing the pairs caused a great debate. Mrs Baldwin's view was clear. There should be an adult with each child. Charlie and Lizzie disagreed. Not only was the island small, making it virtually impossible to get lost, but it would seem very odd if their parents went their separate ways, each with a child in tow. But Mrs Baldwin was sticking to her guns.

'What were you doing when you were my age?' asked Lizzie, knowing very well.

'I was on an expedition with my parents in Tanzania. They were helping with forest conservation.'

'Isn't that the time poachers attacked you?'

'Those were the days.' She smiled, memories flooding back.

'Mum,' shouted Lizzie, getting her mother's attention again. 'We only want to hide some bags. It won't take long and we can borrow one of your phones if you're worried.'

Mr Baldwin knew better than to say anything. This was his wife's decision.

After a long pause, the answer finally came.

'OK. But you must take a phone, and if there are any problems, you must let us know at once.'

'Thanks, Mum.'

'And Charlie, you're in charge. Any mucking about and you'll both be in serious trouble. We'll meet back here in two hours, maximum.'

The children nodded.

With everything decided and rucksacks at the ready, Mr Baldwin took one last glimpse at the chest in the cupboard.

'If that won't put them off, nothing will,' he said, putting a pair of Charlie's underpants on top of the pile. 'Right, let's check out the map. Your mother and I will stay on the west side of the island and you stay on the east.'

As soon as they had locked and double checked the doors and windows, the Baldwin parents waltzed off into the distance. As they disappeared, Lizzie posed a question to Charlie.

'Where is the last place you'd search for hidden treasure if you were Catweazle?'

'Hmm. In or near my hut?'

'Exactly! He's the only one who knows our secret, and I don't think anyone would dare go near there. You remember what Burty said? If you don't bother him, then he won't bother you. If everybody thinks that, then it should be really safe.'

'But Mum and Dad told us to stay away.' Charlie was deep in thought. He couldn't get away from the fact that Lizzie was right. It really was the last place Catweazle would look. 'Ok, agreed. Let's try to find him first so we're watching him and not the other way round.'

Their decision made, the children strode off to Gravedigger's Bay and towards the excavation site. Every few minutes, they would take a quick detour off the track and wait to ensure they weren't being followed.

The news of the burial site had spread across the entire island like wildfire, causing quite a stir. Given this, it quite surprised the children that nobody seemed inquisitive enough to venture over to the bay to see what was going on. But one thing the children were pretty sure of, Catweazle would be somewhere nearby; there was too much going on, what with the Wolfes still plugging away at their end of the beach and Blue and his team in the middle.

As they approached the bay, the children took extra care. They had agreed beforehand that Charlie was to check forward and to their left and Lizzie forward and to their right. Their eyes peeled, they crept along. They approached the excavation site first, but not directly, coming in from the west. From here, they made an arc around it at the distance Catweazle would usually keep watch from. Once they had completed a thorough search of this area, they moved towards the Wolfes' site.

Progress was painfully slow, but they knew from experience that although it was time-consuming, it gave them the best chance of avoiding detection. Once they hit the next danger zone, they moved once again in an arc. They were about midway around the site when Lizzie held up her hand to stop and pointed towards a tree some forty yards away. There, crouched down, was Catweazle.

The children needed to talk, so Charlie pointed in the direction they had come from. Once they had retreated a suitable distance, Charlie checked that Lizzie remembered precisely where the hut was.

'Of course I do. This won't take long. I'll be back in five minutes. If he moves, come and get me or do one of your really loud whistles and I'll meet you by the excavation site. There are a few people there, so we'll be out of harm's way.'

Lizzie shot off and Charlie returned to the place where they had first seen Catweazle. He hadn't moved an inch, so Charlie settled down and waited for Lizzie's return.

The hut wasn't quite where Lizzie remembered, but she found it eventually. She thought about having another look inside, but common sense and memories of the last time won out, and she continued with the task at hand. There was a fair bit of rubbish dotted about, mainly comprising things retrieved from the beach, like fenders and mooring buoys still attached to ropes. There were even a couple of rather tatty looking lobster pots, both with so many holes in that catching anything would be a virtual impossibility. It didn't appear like they'd been moved in years, so Lizzie pushed one of them aside and dug a hole. Pleased, she popped the bag in. Once she'd filled the hole and moved the pot back over it, she dispersed the rest of the sand over the surrounding area. She stood back and admired her efforts. It looked just as it had before.

Charlie kept looking over his shoulder for Lizzie's return, and as soon as she was in sight, he ran back to meet her. Lizzie gave him the spade and explained exactly where to go. With that, she took up the lookout duty and Charlie moved off.

Lizzie hadn't been there long when a tap on the shoulder almost gave her a heart attack.

'What are you doing here?' Blue asked.

'I'm hiding from Charlie. Have you seen him?'

'No, but if I do, I won't say a word.' He gave Lizzie a wink and carried on back to the site.

Lizzie looked back in Catweazle's direction; he was gone!

With Blue so close, Lizzie was loath to whistle immediately, so she waited until he was almost out of sight before she turned, pursing her lips. Charlie had, ever since Lizzie could remember, the ability to whistle incredibly loudly using his fingers. Lizzie had never mastered this, and so had to make do with a far quieter alternative. She was almost certain Charlie wouldn't be able to hear her, so she moved as fast as she could in the hut's direction whilst continuing to whistle.

Charlie meanwhile, under the illusion that he had time to hunt around for somewhere to hide his bag, was looking for somewhere exceptional. It annoyed him he had forgotten to ask Lizzie where she had hidden hers, but no matter, he was sure he could find somewhere equally good, if not better. Happy in the knowledge that she was keeping a lookout and that he was safe for the time being, he once again ventured into the hut. Nothing really stuck out, but the floor was only sand, so he looked for a decent spot. In the far corner were the steel rods which Catweazle had purloined a few days ago. His mind was made up. Charlie moved the rods and started digging as fast as he could. As he put the bag in the hole, something caught his attention. In the distance, he could hear whistling, and it was getting louder. He had to move fast. He covered the bag, put the poles back in precisely the same position that he had found them, and scattered the remaining sand. Then he made a hasty move for the door. This time Catweazle was ready and grabbed Charlie by the scruff of the neck.

130

Chapter 16:   Now They All Know

'What are you doing here?' said Catweazle, drawing Charlie's face so close he could smell his rancid breath.

Charlie stared, eyes like saucepans, into his unblinking eyes.

'I said, what are you doing here?' Charlie felt the fine droplets of saliva hit his skin as Catweazle continued his rant.

'I came back for the rods.'

'I don't believe you. I think you have something of mine and I want it back.'

Struggling was futile. Although thin, Catweazle was immensely strong, and he held Charlie in a vice-like grip.

'Where is it? I want to know. You can't just come here,' and he stopped mid-sentence as something whacked him extremely hard behind the knees.

'Aargh,' he cried in pain as he dropped to the ground, letting Charlie go in the process.

'Come on, we need to get back to Blue,' yelled Lizzie, throwing the piece of wood to the ground.

Charlie didn't need a second prompt, and in an instant, he was charging through the trees with Lizzie close at his heels. Catweazle got to his feet and attempted to make chase. But Lizzie had hit him hard, and after a few paces he accepted defeat. With one last glance at the children, he turned and hobbled back to his hut. He needed to find out what Charlie had really been up to.

At the excavation site, the children had time to gather their wits about them. Charlie looked at the phone. Time had been ticking away faster than they thought; it was almost time to meet their parents. They set off at a jog, giving Catweazle's hut as wide a berth as possible and sticking to the path. With any luck, he was still licking his wounds at home.

Just over fifteen minutes later, and with a great sense of relief, they were back in their parents' company.

'Right, let's have some lunch,' said Mrs Baldwin, rising from her chair.

'Good idea,' replied the other three in unison.

Over lunch, the children told their story. It surprised them that their parents didn't show a more sympathetic attitude. After all, Lizzie had shown immense courage. In fact, quite the opposite, they were extremely angry. The children had disobeyed them and put themselves in unnecessary danger.

'Your father told you not to go back there.'

'I did. How would you react if you found someone poking around our house?'

'But he had Charlie by the neck and what if...'

'If you'd listened to us, you wouldn't have been there in the first place.'

'Lizzie saved my life!' Charlie knew he was exaggerating, but he had to defend his sister after what she had just done for him.

As the conversation became increasingly heated and voices raised, Mrs Baldwin thought it time to draw a line under it.

'You were extremely brave, Lizzie, but you really shouldn't have been anywhere near Catweazle's. Now let's not hear another word about it. Next time, please do as we say.'

'But it was a good place to hide the bags.'

'Elizabeth!' said her mother, with an expression telling her that this was the final word.

Once they'd finished eating and were back in their rooms, Mr Baldwin got out his map. He showed the children his crosses, marking the locations of the gold they had hidden. In their excitement, Charlie and Lizzie had completely forgotten to ask how their parents got on. They could see from their father's face that he was rather pleased with himself and was very keen to tell all.

Five minutes later, the children were asking themselves if they had ever heard a more boring story. Their parents had enjoyed a trouble-free walk that morning, during which, away from the general population, they buried their bags of gold. What on earth was exciting about that?

Next came the bombshell that their parents thought it a good idea to retrace their footsteps so they could show the children exactly where they had hidden the bags. The children had envisaged a much more enjoyable afternoon at Gravedigger's Bay, watching the Wolfe party digging up the beach in vain. But there was no argument. They thought it better to get back in their parents' good books.

The route they took was very familiar, as it was the one they had taken a couple of days before to get to Yeaman's Bay. This time, however, rather than turning right and heading towards the bay, they carried on down the road. To be fair, the trip proved slightly less boring than they had imagined from their father's story. They saw various colourful birds and lizards on the way and a rather mangy looking dog which crossed the road immediately in front of them. Everyone kept well clear as it looked pretty wild, but it just glanced at them momentarily and then went about its business. Finally, they came to a very wild-looking area on their right with a sign saying "Stay Away, Enter at Your Peril".

'That's different,' said Charlie.

'We thought so too,' said his father.

A rather dilapidated wooden fence bordered the land, probably erected at the same time as the sign if appearances were anything to go by. Angled down to its left, with weather-beaten edges and faded writing, it bore the marks of both age and neglect. To the right of the sign would have been a gate, but it was now long gone and in its place there was some rather grotty rope tied between the two, far from upright, gateposts. Beyond the rope, although hard to make out amongst all the undergrowth, were the remnants of an old track.

'Come on then,' said Mr Baldwin as he held the rope up for his wife to duck under.

'But the sign,' said Lizzie.

134

'Don't be daft. Look at it. Nobody's touched it in years. Whoever wrote it will be long gone by now.'

With their father's seal of approval, the children nipped under the rope and they carried on up the path.

'We thought it looked very wild,' said Mr Baldwin, 'and with the sign and everything, the bags should be pretty safe.'

'Here we are.' Mrs Baldwin kicked aside some rather thin undergrowth to reveal a freshly dug area of ground.

'We shouldn't linger. I've marked the spot by putting two small rocks by that tree.' Mr Baldwin turned and winked at Charlie and Lizzie. 'Right, let's carry on.'

Another twenty paces up the track, they called the children to a halt.

'It's under there,' said Mr Baldwin.

The children followed his gaze to a large rock a few yards to the left-hand side of the track.

'Don't worry, it moves relatively easily. Now, let's get back. We don't want to hang around too long.'

'Can you hear music?' Lizzie asked, a puzzled look on her face.

They all stopped and listened. Sure enough, the faint sound of song floated all around.

'It sounds like someone singing a sea shanty,' said their mother, 'but we're in the middle of nowhere, so it can't be. I'm sure there's a completely logical explanation.'

'Probably the wind in the trees, or perhaps even a passing yacht if it has got its music blaring away,' suggested Mr Baldwin.

The wind changed direction and once again, all fell silent.

Back at Burty's, Mr Baldwin had a quick glance in their cupboard to check nothing was amiss. He let out a huge sigh of relief as he saw the pile of dirty laundry exactly where they had left it. Now that they had hidden the bags, he was loath to wander too far off with something so valuable in the room, so he suggested to everyone that they hang around Burty's for the rest of the afternoon while he mulled over what to do. Charlie and Lizzie were still full of beans and needed something to do, so their mother agreed to take them to the nearest beach whilst her husband stayed put and read a book.

Just before five o'clock, they arrived back at Burty's. They'd had a great afternoon splashing about in the water, interspersed with some top-level snorkelling. The children told their father with great excitement that they had finally found the elusive lobsters that Tallboy had been talking about, just in a completely different location. Anyway, they would take him there the following afternoon if time allowed. With any luck, they could catch their dinner. They had thought about trying themselves that afternoon, but something about the size of the lobsters' claws had put them off.

It was getting late and Mr Baldwin was getting thirsty, so he suggested that they all get showered and dressed and go for a drink before dinner. The suggestion hit the spot, and not twenty minutes later there they were, washed and dressed, or "abluted and suited", as Mr Baldwin liked to say, ready to go.

They arrived at the bar with a definite spring in their step, and Sandra welcomed them and asked them how their day had been.

'Great thanks, Sandra,' said Lizzie. 'We saw loads of lobsters when we were snorkelling. We might go back tomorrow and try to get some for dinner.'

'That sounds a great idea. I'll tell chef to hold off with his menu, just in case.'

They were all sitting there waiting for Sandra to come and take their orders when she arrived with two rum punches and two lemonades.

'There you go.'

'Thank you, Sandra, that's perfect,' said Mrs Baldwin.

'Shall we eat at The Grand this evening?' asked Mr Baldwin. With everyone's minds elsewhere, nobody said a word. 'Well, that's settled then.'

After another round of drinks, all drunk at a leisurely pace, they set off across the road and a couple of minutes later, were being seated at a table on the terrace. There was a warm, cooling breeze going out to sea, and they sat there watching the last few yachts coming in to moor for the night. There were a few shouts coming from the boats and the children watched intently, waiting for something to happen, but annoyingly nothing did.

Drinks in hand, Mr Baldwin raised his glass and made a toast to what so far had been an incredible holiday. He was about to put his glass down on the table when he raised it again to acknowledge some people at another table. As the children turned to see who it was, the raised glasses and piercing stares of the Wolfe brothers met their eyes.

An hour and a half later, with their dinner finished and paid for, the Baldwin family got up to leave. As they walked into the atrium from the terrace, Lizzie, who was busy talking to Charlie, bumped into a gentleman returning from the toilets. The impact, although not great, was large enough to knock something from Lizzie's hand, which made a heavy clunk as it hit the floor. The gentleman bent down and picked it up.

'I do apologise,' said Peregrine (or was it Edward) Wolfe, 'it was entirely my fault.'

He gently tossed the coin in the palm of his hand, feeling the weight. He seemed mesmerised by it. Slowly turning it with his thumb and forefinger, he took in every detail. It all happened so fast that there was nothing any of the Baldwins could do. After what seemed like an eternity to Lizzie, he held out his hand.

'There you are.'

'Thank you.'

'My pleasure, and I'm sure we'll be seeing each other again soon.' Sooner than they could ever imagine. And a sinister smile flashed across his face.

Chapter 17:   Questions, Questions

The Baldwins stood there in silence, under no illusion that their secret was out.

Then, after a long pause, Mr Baldwin responded. 'We'll look forward to it. Enjoy the rest of your evening.'

'Thank you, you too,' came the reply as he turned and headed off back to his table.

Once back in their rooms, before anybody had time to say anything, Lizzie offered her most sincere apologies. She appreciated just how stupid she had been. She'd put the coin in her pocket on the first evening, not that it was much of an excuse.

'We can't turn back the clock, so there's no use crying over spilt milk,' said Mr Baldwin.

'My worry is the Wolfes,' said Charlie. 'Whichever one of them picked it up not only saw it, but knows it's genuine. Don't forget how heavy they are.'

'What are the Wolfes doing here, anyway?' asked Mrs Baldwin.

The children felt that this was as good a time as any to come clean with their parents, so told them the entire story from the very beginning, starting with the discovery of the map.

'So the story you told us at Granny's was true. It sounded so far-fetched,' said Mr Baldwin. 'I'm so sorry I didn't believe you.'

'But we found the treasure, didn't we Lizzie?' said Charlie, looking at his sister, beaming away.

Mr Baldwin couldn't believe how lucky they had been to make their discovery. If it hadn't been for the box he'd hidden, the children would probably still be digging.

'So correct me if I'm wrong. The Wolfes know that we've found precisely what they are here for, too. They have gone to quite some expense, so I doubt they are going to just leave it at that. Then there is Catweazle. He knows we've got something, but I can't imagine he knows exactly what. I'd say it's about time we told Blue what we've found before things get serious.'

'That would be best, what with Catweazle in the children's room and nobody having the faintest idea what the Wolfes are going to do now,' said Mrs Baldwin. 'Mind you, they won't know what hit them if they come into my room,' she continued, taking everyone by surprise.

'Does that mean we must give the treasure away for ever?' asked Lizzie.

'Hopefully not,' replied her father. 'Even back home, you've got to report any treasure you find, so it shouldn't be the last we see of it.'

With the course of action agreed, they settled down for the night, but not before locking the doors and windows and then checking everything once again. There was only one night to go now that they had made their decision to let Blue in on their not so little secret.

The children woke at daybreak only to find their father already up, dressed and sitting on a chair outside his room.

'I couldn't sleep, not after the other night and Catweazle. Too much on my mind.'

'There was a lot of snoring for someone who couldn't sleep,' said his wife.

'Every little noise woke me up. I kept thinking someone was trying to break in. Anyway, everything is exactly where we left it, so as soon as you're all ready for breakfast, I'll find Burty and ask for Blue's number or the best place to find him at this time of day.'

Twenty minutes later, they left their rooms. Mr Baldwin locked and double-checked each door and window, before setting off towards Reception to find Burty. Meanwhile, Mrs Baldwin and the children carried on to the restaurant for breakfast.

'Morning Burty, do you know how I can get hold of Blue?'

'Good morning. Sure, you can telephone him, but it will probably be easier to go to his house. He's only a couple of minutes' walk from here. What do you need to talk to Blue for? Is there a problem? Anything I can help you with?'

'Nothing major. There was someone in the children's room the other night. I wanted to report it.'

Burty was bolt upright in an instant and looking at Mr Baldwin, flabbergasted. 'It must have been a visitor. I'm sure it wouldn't have been someone from the island. You should have told me straight away.'

'You're right, I'm sorry. We think it might have been Catweazle, though.'

'What would Catweazle want with you?' His brow furrowed as he stroked his chin.

'Beats me.'

Burty stood there in silence, deep in thought. Mr Baldwin could see that he sensed something wasn't quite right. Then, after what felt like an age, he continued.

'Just turn left out of the main door, take the first road on your left, and you will see the police station on your right-hand side after a minute or two. The station is part of Blue's house, so he should be there somewhere. It's still quite early.'

'Ah yes, we've passed the Police Station on our travels.' Mr Baldwin thanked Burty for his help and joined the rest of the family for breakfast.

Once finished, they got up and, rather than going back to their rooms, headed out of the front door en masse and went in search of Blue. They knew exactly where he lived. The police station was hard to miss with its enormous blue and white sign.

Mr Baldwin rang the bell, and it wasn't long before the door swung open to reveal Blue standing there in his boxer shorts.

'Good morning, Mr Baldwin. How can I help you?'

'Good morning Blue, sorry it's so early. Someone broke into the children's room and we thought you should know. May we come in?'

Blue opened the door and led them through to the office.

142

'Take a seat. I'm just going to get into uniform; this is police business!'

As before, he sounded rather excited. It seemed that every time they spoke to him, the more he was escaping from his rather normal, dreary, crime free routine.

On his return, he sat down, opened a notebook, and took a pen from his drawer.

'So, you say someone broke into your room? When was this?'

'A couple of nights ago. He didn't really break in, more like clambered through an open window,' said Charlie.

'If it was a couple of nights ago, why didn't you come and inform me sooner?'

'It was only Catweazle, at least that's what we think. So we didn't really worry,' replied Mr Baldwin.

'That sounds quite unlikely. Are you sure it was him?'

'Let me start at the beginning,' said Mr Baldwin. He told Blue the entire story, from finding the treasure chest to taking it back to their room and hiding it in the cupboard. He also mentioned that as far as he was aware, Catweazle didn't know exactly what they had discovered, so was probably there to find out, which he had failed to do.

'So why didn't you report your discovery immediately?'

'We weren't sure what to do,' replied Mr Baldwin. 'We were so excited all we wanted to do initially was keep it safe, which we have done.'

Blue explained exactly what they should have done, and listened to a rather embarrassed Mr Baldwin make his excuses. But he could see that there was no ill intention in the course of action they had taken, so he finished his report on a favourable note. He had grown quite fond of the family who had brought him from relative obscurity to the front page of The Gazette. This latest discovery could mean international recognition, imagine!

'Right, let's go and see exactly what we have.'

A few minutes later, they arrived back at Burty's. They could hear Sandra singing to herself in the kitchen, but other than that, all was quiet. As they approached their rooms, Mr Baldwin reached in his pocket for the key. He tried to turn it anticlockwise in the lock to open the door, but it met with resistance.

'Let me try,' said Blue.

He tried first one way and then the other. There was a click, and he pulled down the handle and pushed the door to open it. It was locked. He turned it back and tried again. The door opened.

'You'd forgotten to lock it,' he said.

There was a great deal of commotion as the children ran past Blue and opened the cupboard. There, where the chest should have been, was a pile of dirty laundry. Charlie's heart sank, and his stomach twisted and turned uncontrollably. Things whizzed around in his head at a million miles an hour. The gold would have solved all of their problems. They had to find it again, they just had to. As soon as he got the chance, he'd let Lizzie know about their father's

144

situation and why getting the treasure back was so important. He needed her focused.

'I definitely locked the door, and I double-checked everything before we left for breakfast,' said Mr Baldwin.

Blue looked at them, puzzled.

'There is no sign of anyone breaking in and, more to the point, there is no sign of any chest. Even if I believe you, I really have nothing at all to go on.'

'Someone must have used a key. Let's ask Burty how many keys there are and who has access to them.'

Blue could see in their faces they were distraught, so he gave them the benefit of the doubt and they went to find Burty.

'He's doing the shopping,' said Sandra, who was busy washing up in the kitchen. 'As far as I'm aware, there are only two spare sets of keys. Burty keeps one lot in the safe, and the others are on hooks in the office so that the cleaner can use them.'

'Can you show me where exactly?' asked Blue.

Sandra took him round the back of the reception desk and through the office door. Sure enough, there was a long row of hooks, each one with a room number above, and there were keys on every hook.

'Can I help you at all?' asked Burty as he walked back past Reception, bags of food in hand. 'Let me just put these in the kitchen.'

A minute later, Burty was back, greeting Blue with a smile and a handshake.

Blue explained the Baldwins had come to him about someone being in their room. When he had come back to see if there was any evidence of this, they had found the room unlocked, even though Mr Baldwin was certain that he had locked the door before he had left.

'There are only two other keys,' said Burty. 'One's there on the hook and the other's in the safe over here.'

He walked across the room and entered the code.

'There we are,' he said, pulling out an enormous bunch of keys. 'There is one thing, Blue. Mr Baldwin mentioned to me he thought Catweazle might have been the person in the children's room, but I just can't imagine it. I know you've only been on the island a couple of years, but I've been here for nearer fifty and have known Catweazle all my life. Not to talk to of late, but it just doesn't seem like something he'd do. He steers well clear of people, watches, but steers clear.'

Blue didn't want to divulge too much. The last thing he needed if the story of the treasure was true was a lot of unwanted interest hampering his investigations. For the time being, he would keep the conversation back in the police station strictly between him and the Baldwins.

'Hmm. Thanks for your help, Burty. Right, let's go back to your room and I'll take a few notes down and try to wrap this up for today,' he said, wanting some privacy.

Once back in the room, having had more time to mull things over, Blue continued.

'Are you certain that you locked the door?' he said, looking at Mr Baldwin.

'Absolutely certain.'

'I want to believe you about the treasure, but without evidence that it was here, or even existed, it will be very hard for me to pursue any line of enquiry or engage additional help.'

Blue looked very disappointed. He had wanted to get his teeth stuck into an actual crime ever since he arrived on the island, and this would have been the perfect case. A mystery involving hidden treasure. What more could he have asked for?

Charlie leant over to Lizzie and whispered something in her ear. Lizzie nodded and reached deep into her pocket. She stood up and walked towards Blue, who was still jotting down notes.

She held out her hand and dropped the doubloon squarely in the middle of the notebook.

'Now this changes everything,' said Blue, beaming from ear to ear.

Chapter 18:   The Finger Points Where?

They all agreed not to utter a word about the treasure. It was a small island, and they didn't want the entire population pointing accusing fingers everywhere. That would only confuse the issue. Blue needed time to go over everything. He also needed to make sure that the excavation carried on unhindered. People would start asking what was going on if anything slowed down the most important discovery on the island for years.

Blue asked the Baldwins if they could remember anything suspicious they might have seen. They should also make a note of everyone they'd met since their arrival. They would all meet back at the police station at 5pm. This would give Blue time to sort everything out from his side and the Baldwins time to think.

As deflated as they felt, thoughts of solving the great mystery with Blue soon lifted their spirits. If truth be known, they were all quite relieved that they no longer had the treasure and were now the hunters and not the hunted.

With all the excitement, it was already mid-morning before they set off. As it was getting late, they stopped at Eglit's Emporium on the way to grab a few supplies rather than ask Sandra to make anything for them.

A more relaxed mood descended on the entire family, and it took almost twice as long as normal before they finally set down their things on the beach at Gravedigger's Bay.

As they looked around, they spotted a few things that were different. Firstly, there was absolutely no sign of the Wolfes or their henchmen, and secondly, the excavation of the burial site seemed to have continued unabated. There were now some twenty skeletons lying there side by side. On a positive note, Blue had decided not to cordon off the entire beach, not for the time being, anyway.

'I'm going to find out how they are getting on,' said Charlie. 'Are you coming, Lizzie?'

With a nod of her head, they leapt up and began walking over to where the latest round of digging was going on.

'What's wrong Charlie? You haven't really said a thing since Blue left this morning.'

Charlie could see that now was as good a time as any to spill the beans.

'I've got something to tell you, Lizzie, but you must promise to keep it to yourself.' Charlie fiddled with his fingers, and from his deadpan look, Lizzie could see it was serious.

'Cross my heart.' The smile had disappeared from Lizzie's face, too.

'It looks like we've got to move house, at least if we don't get the chest back.' Charlie hesitated for an instant. 'Dad's lost his job.'

'But we still have the jewels from the box,' Lizzie said hesitantly.

'We do, but gold is worth a fortune, and the chest is full of it.'

'And if we don't find it?'

'Look, Lizzie, we HAVE to find it. I don't want to move. We can't even be sure if we'll stay in the same area. It might mean new schools, the lot.'

The enormity of what she had just heard suddenly hit home, and Lizzie's eyes filled with tears. 'But our friends.'

'I know Lizzie. That's why we have to get it back. For you, for me, and for Mum and Dad.'

Lizzie dried her eyes with the back of her hand. This wasn't the time for tears. She had to focus.

When they returned, they told their parents that the excavation team had now uncovered twenty-two skeletons. Once certain that they had found everything, they would take a photograph of them all in situ and take them off for analysis. As soon as they had any definite news, they would let them know.

Mr and Mrs Baldwin had, in the meantime, started making the list of people they'd met. They were thankful that they had kept themselves to themselves as they finished the list in no time. They showed it to the children and asked them if they remembered anyone else or if they had met someone that they didn't know about.

'Well, you've forgotten Sandra,' said Charlie. A grin came over everyone's face. Nobody in their right mind could imagine Sandra having anything to do with it, which is probably why she hadn't sprung to mind. Other than that, they all agreed that the list seemed to be complete.

They had a relaxing day at the beach, interspersed with various theories of who the culprit or culprits were. But it was proving difficult to drag their minds away from Catweazle and the Wolfe brothers. After all, these were the only suspects who knew about their find.

It was then that they remarked upon the fact that nobody had seen Catweazle all day. OK, they hadn't been keeping a close eye out for him, but they normally sensed when he was about, but they felt nothing of the sort today.

After lunch, Charlie took Lizzie aside. He suggested that they have a look around Catweazle's hut for the chest. It was big and so difficult to hide, especially given the limited number of things he owned. Lizzie resisted, worried about going against their parents' orders. She was also more than a little scared. Charlie reminded her they hadn't seen Catweazle all day, and anyway, their parents weren't always right.

'Alright, if you're sure it'll be safe. But only if I keep lookout and you do the snooping about.'

'Deal.'

Charlie shouted to their parents. He and Lizzie were off hunting in the woods. It showed how much more relaxed they were, letting them wander off given what had gone on before. They didn't even ask what they were hunting for.

The children, now familiar with the area, crept directly to Catweazle's hut. This time, they stuck well and truly together. Lizzie scanned the area constantly whilst Charlie searched everywhere. He hesitated somewhat before opening the door, but he took a deep breath and slowly swung it open. Nothing seemed out of place as far as he could see, with the rods still standing where he had left them. As quickly as they had arrived, they left, leaving everything exactly as they found it.

The children didn't feel too disheartened by the lack of treasure. Once they had involved the police, a thorough search of Catweazle's property became inevitable, so it made little sense for him to keep it there.

After a rather restful afternoon, in which Mrs Baldwin only paused from her reading for the occasional drink and something to eat, they tidied up their belongings and began the trek back to town. The children and their father had come up with every theory under the sun, but nearly every time it came back to the brothers. Whatever angle Blue was taking, they were going to have to do some digging of their own in the Wolfes' direction.

As arranged, they stopped in at the police station on the way home to find Blue frantically scribbling notes on a whiteboard.

'Welcome, I'm glad you're all here. Have you got the list of names?'

'Here it is,' said Mr Baldwin, passing it across.

'Thanks. I'm writing the names of all the suspects up on the board and I'm crossing them off one by one as they give me their alibis and I confirm them.'

He was in his element, but Mrs Baldwin couldn't help but think that it was his first time carrying out an investigation like this. It looked like he had got most of his detective work theory from the television.

'Right, the list. Are there any people on the list who, in your eyes, are more suspicious than the others?'

'Catweazle and the Wolfe brothers!' blurted out Lizzie, unable to contain herself.

Blue knew about their reasons for suspecting Catweazle, but Edward and Peregrine Wolfe would need some explaining.

Charlie and Lizzie, to Blue's great interest, told their story right from the beginning, from when they had first found the map in the drawer.

'What a story. So where's the other treasure?'

'We still have it,' said Lizzie. 'You saw us with it on the beach, if you remember.'

'I'll explain about that later, if you don't mind,' said Mr Baldwin. 'Let's concentrate on the one that's missing.'

Blue realised that this was something Mr Baldwin wanted to discuss with him alone and obligingly changed the discussion back to the stolen treasure.

'It does all sound a bit too much of a coincidence with the Wolfes. They spot a gold coin one evening and the treasure goes missing the very next day.'

'And there's still Catweazle,' said Charlie.

'From what you've said, I think it's unlikely to be Catweazle. The chest sounds too heavy for a single man to carry, so he would need an accomplice. If he'd dragged it on his own, we would have seen the marks.'

'I can assure you, he's very strong,' remarked Charlie.

Blue ignored this. He was now in a world of his own. 'And if you're certain you locked the door, that would mean that someone took the key from the office to open the door, entered your room, took the chest and then calmly put the key back on its hook. All this without being noticed.'

When he said it like that, it did all seem rather unlikely.

'Anyway, I'll let you go now. I need to figure things out. Thanks for your help and let me know if you think of anything else or you see anyone acting suspiciously.'

'We will do, and thanks,' said Mr Baldwin as he rose from his chair.

As the others left, he turned. 'I just need a quick word with Blue. I'll catch you up in a mo.' He closed the door and explained about the other treasure.

'Let's go for a drink at The Grand,' said Mrs Baldwin to the children. 'I'd like to see what the Wolfes are up to.'

'Can we wait for Dad?' said Charlie.

Lizzie could see by his manner that he had thought of something.

Back at Burty's, Mrs Baldwin sat in the warmth of the disappearing sun, reading her book.

'Lizzie and I are going off exploring.'

'Don't wander too far and be back here in thirty minutes.'

Charlie grabbed his sister and headed off to Reception. Sandra was knitting away behind the desk.

'Could we have an envelope if you've got a spare one please, Sandra?' said Charlie.

She rummaged around under the desk before handing them a small envelope. 'There you go.'

'Could you do me a favour and write "E and P Wolfe" on it, please?'

'I don't know what you children are up to, but sure,' she replied, smiling. She'd never even heard of E and P Wolfe, so what was it to her?

'Thanks, Sandra, you're a star,' and Charlie, closely followed by Lizzie, ran across the road to The Grand.

'Check the Wolfes aren't here,' he said to Lizzie in a hushed voice. They split up and busied themselves with looking around the bar and terrace area for the two brothers.

'I can't see them,' said Lizzie.

'Me neither.'

Confident they were alone, Charlie went to Reception and held out the envelope.

'Can I leave this for the Wolfes, please?'

'Certainly, young man.'

The smartly dressed receptionist took the envelope, turned around and put it in the cubbyhole behind her, marked Room 112.

'Thanks,' said Charlie. His plan had worked.

Chapter 19: A Magical Island

As they left The Grand, Lizzie congratulated Charlie on his brilliance. They, or rather he, had found out the number of the Wolfes' room, without even asking! All they had to do now was get in there undetected and search for clues as to the whereabouts of the chest. They wouldn't have enough time now, and anyway, they didn't know whether the Wolfes were in their room, making it far too dangerous for the time being. Better to give it some thought before trying anything.

They walked back into Burty's and spotted their father just ahead of them.

'Hey, Dad,' Charlie yelled, 'wait for us.'

Mr Baldwin turned around and smiled. They might not have the gold, but this was turning out to be one heck of a holiday.

Drinks at The Grand were quite uneventful, for the parents anyway. Charlie and Lizzie, having spotted the Wolfe brothers at another table, executed the first part of their plan.

'I'm just off to the toilet,' said Charlie, winking at Lizzie.

He wandered off toward the Gents, turning to have a good look around as he got there. No-one was close by, so he carried on past the door and disappeared out of sight around the corner. A few minutes later, he returned, giving Lizzie a discrete thumbs up as he approached. Mission accomplished.

'Another drink, anyone?' said Mr Baldwin as he finished his rum punch.

'I'm sorry to say I'm ravenous as usual,' said his wife. 'Can we go back to Burty's and have dinner?'

The bill paid, they rose from their seats and turned towards the door. It was interesting. The Wolfes had been so deep in discussion they hadn't even spotted they were there. Mind you, it was far better that way. They didn't want them watching their every move.

Following dinner and back in the privacy of their room, the children got to work.

'It's perfect,' said Charlie, 'room 112 is on the ground floor facing the sea.'

'When shall we go?'

'Now's as good a time as any.'

They tiptoed to the door and made a dash for it.

They knew the area like the backs of their hands by now. Once they had checked that the Wolfes were still at their table, they would creep round to their room and see if there was any sign of the treasure. The children entered the hotel, calmly chatting amongst themselves, and when nobody was looking, slipped through a side door into the garden.

To their relief, Peregrine and Edward Wolfe were in full view of the garden, sitting there, heads together, chatting away. They each had a semi-full glass of red wine, so the children knew there was no hurry. They carried on around the perimeter of the lawn, as far out of sight as possible, with Charlie counting the doors and terraces of the rooms as they progressed.

157

'This side started at room 107, so it will be the sixth one down.'

It was getting late, and they only saw one couple sitting at a small table outside their room. Thankfully, a small hedge separated each terrace, providing the children with an element of cover.

As they approached room 112, they noticed that the bedside lamps were still on. Although it allowed them an initial insight into what lay in store, it also meant that they would have to take extra care once inside. With the lights on, anyone in the garden could see them through the window. As they peered in, the number of suits and other unsuitable holiday attire confirmed it was most definitely the right room.

The Wolfes had left a window ajar to keep the air circulating. It was one of the upper windows, so Charlie gave Lizzie a leg up, she being the lighter and smaller of the two. She flicked it open and wriggled through. It was a tricky manoeuvre, made more difficult by the lack of help on the inside. But she kept a tight hold of the frame, swung her legs round and jumped to the floor.

With a turn of the latch, Lizzie opened the door. Charlie scanned around to check the coast was clear, then entered, closing the door behind him.

It didn't take long to look round the room, as although it was large, there wasn't anywhere to hide anything. They checked in the cupboard first and then under the beds. Here they found two identical leather suitcases, beautifully embossed with the initials, PW and EW. Charlie pulled them out and he and Lizzie found it difficult to contain their laughter when they opened them. Not only were the suitcases identical, but so were their contents: black socks, Y-front pants, string vests, a nightshirt and opened packets of mothballs.

'That explains their rather unique smell,' laughed Charlie.

'And who brings a vest to the Caribbean?'

They shut the suitcases and slid them back under the beds. It was time to go.

But there was a problem. They hadn't thought quite how to get out. Actually, leaving was easy, but doing it without a trace was another thing entirely. If one of them exited via the door and the other locked it, then who would be there to help him or her back through the window?

Charlie had an idea and crept to the main door. He turned the doorknob and smiled. Bingo, they could open it from the inside.

'Hurry Lizzie, put the window back on the latch and lock the door and let's get out of here.'

Lizzie did what she was told and ran to the door. Charlie eased it open and peered through the crack to check it was all clear. He was just about to leave when he heard the voices of the Wolfe brothers as they turned into the passage.

'They're coming, Lizzie, quick, hide.'

Charlie shut the door, and they made a dash for it, sliding beneath the beds and out of sight just as the door opened. One brother walked within touching distance of Lizzie, slipping his shoes off and kicking them under the bed. One of them whacked her square on the nose, and although she stayed silent, her eyes watered uncontrollably, everything becoming a blur.

'Nightcap?' said Peregrine (or was it Edward) to his brother.

'Oh, go on then,' came the reply as his brother grabbed a bottle of rum and two glasses.

To Lizzie's relief, they moved onto the terrace, giving her the opportunity for a short, sharp sniff. One of the brothers turned momentarily towards the room before pulling out his chair and joining his sibling at the table. Once they had settled down and were back in deep conversation, Charlie gestured to Lizzie, who was only just regaining her focus. He put a finger to his lips, then pointed to the door. As one, they scrambled as quickly and quietly from under their beds as they could.

Charlie fixed his eyes on the brothers, still busy talking away.

'Nibbles?' said one of them, pushing his chair back and getting to his feet.

Charlie and Lizzie crouched down beside the beds as he entered the room. He grabbed a packet of peanuts from a small basket on the side and turned.

'Sure?'

'I'm fine, thanks. Now let's get back to business.'

His attention elsewhere, he returned to his chair, oblivious to the children's presence.

Lizzie looked at her brother, his eyes wide-open and face blank. She motioned towards the door. A moment later, he nodded. Still crouching, they made their way to the exit. Charlie turned the knob painfully slowly. Now wasn't the time to panic. As soon as they had a sufficient gap, Lizzie slipped out, closely followed by her brother. Once outside, he closed the door as carefully as possible. With one final, and to the children, deafening click, it locked.

'Did you hear that?'

'It must have come from someone else's room. You can't open these doors from the outside without a key.'

The brothers gave a casual glance round and continued with their planning.

As the children got back to the entrance hall, they gave enormous sighs of relief.

'That was too close for comfort,' said Lizzie, taking a few deep breaths.

'Agreed. Part of me wanted to stay longer and listen to what they were talking about, but when he came back in I just froze.'

The children continued chatting as they got ready for bed, but the day's events had once again taken their toll, both mentally and physically, so it wasn't long before they were both fast asleep.

It was Mr Baldwin who was up at the crack of dawn the following day. He'd slept very well, but once awake had got to thinking about what had gone on so far and whether there was anything else they could do to speed up the investigation. With no-one else awake, he grabbed a towel and sauntered off to the nearest beach for an early morning dip.

By the time he returned, there was movement from all quarters, so as soon as everyone was ready, they started their daily routine and headed off for breakfast. As they passed reception, Burty popped his head up from behind the desk.

'Good morning, you lovely people.'

'Good morning, Burty,' they replied in unison.

'And what plans do you have for today?'

'Nothing in particular,' said Mr Baldwin. 'We might go on another voyage of discovery. In fact, I've been meaning to ask you something. The other day when we were out exploring the island, we saw a sign saying "stay away, enter at your peril". What's all that about? It sounds rather aggressive in this day and age.'

Burty's face turned to stone, and he fell silent.

'It's not another burial site for the victims of dengue fever,' Mr Baldwin continued, trying to lighten the mood but failing badly.

'Don't joke about that place,' said Burty. 'Have you ever heard of voodoo?'

'Of course, witch doctors and all that.'

'Not really. It's more to do with spirits. Be careful, the sign is there to keep people away. The entire area is cursed. Some have been there in the past and never come back.'

By the look on his face, they could see that he was being serious.

'It is said that sometimes people hear music, enticing them in, but no-one has ever lived to tell the tale. It's a place no man should go. My advice is to steer well clear.'

When Burty mentioned the music, it sent a shiver down everyone's spine.

'Well, thanks for that. It's not something we're likely to forget,' said Mr Baldwin.

'My pleasure. Enjoy your breakfast and have a great day,' he said, a smile returning to his face.

Once seated, the conversation was slightly different to the one everyone had imagined when they left their rooms only five minutes earlier.

'Voodoo, what's that?' asked Lizzie.

It soon became apparent that although their parents had ideas about what voodoo was, they clearly didn't know for sure. In fact, according to their mother, most of their father's knowledge seemed to have come from a James Bond film he had seen when he was young. Anyway, it seemed to involve spirits, so until they had discovered more about it, it was something not to take too lightly.

One thing they congratulated themselves on were the places they had hidden the bags of gold. Nobody would ever think of looking at Catweazle's, or beyond the sign from what they had just heard, so they should be perfectly safe for the time being.

They decided en masse that they would take a break from Gravedigger's Bay today, so bags packed, they went off to Eglit's Emporium for some provisions. On the way to the beach, they walked past the police station and saw Blue on his radio out on the veranda.

'I'll speak to you later,' he said, putting the radio down.

'Any news?' asked Mrs Baldwin.

'Nothing yet. They've sent help over from one of the other islands, and my colleague has just found Catweazle. She's bringing him in for questioning. I'm going to talk to the Wolfe brothers later this afternoon.'

'My money's still on the Wolfes,' said Lizzie.

'I'm not discounting anyone until they've given me a cast-iron alibi.'

Mr Baldwin liked this professional approach, but he still had ideas of his own. 'One more thing, Blue. Is there any voodoo practiced on the island you know of?'

'Nobody's ever mentioned it, but I've only been here a couple of years. Probably worth asking a local. Oh, and by the way young lady,' he said, smiling at Lizzie, 'I believe I have something of yours.'

Blue nipped into his office, returning with the doubloon held high between his thumb and forefinger.

'Thank you so much, Blue.' Lizzie was positively beaming as she slipped it back in her pocket.

The day on the beach was a very relaxing one, with some fantastic snorkelling for the children and their father. As for Mrs Baldwin, she welcomed the peace and quiet and sat under the parasol, in her idea of heaven, ploughing through her books as well as most of the food!

There was a lot of discussion regarding who was the guilty party, but it was proving very difficult to come to any agreement. Mrs Baldwin had brought up the point that if Catweazle had stolen the chest, the Wolfes wouldn't know and so would still be searching for it. Equally, if the Wolfes had stolen it, then Catweazle should be oblivious to the fact and still be after it. So they, or at least their rooms, were still potential targets even though they didn't have the chest.

Hopefully, when they got back to Blue's, the mystery would be over. Even if it wasn't, all the suspects would know that he was monitoring them, which made them feel a lot safer.

Then the talk turned to voodoo.

'It's a shame Blue couldn't shed any light on the voodoo,' said Mr Baldwin.

'I bet you I know who can,' said Mrs Baldwin. 'Vin, from Eglit's Emporium, told me his grandfather's 110. They're islanders born and bred, so he'll know more than a hundred years of what's been going on.'

It amazed the children that someone could be so old.

'That means he could be a great-great-grandfather!' exclaimed Lizzie.

'You mean a great-great-great-grandfather,' said Charlie, working it out on his fingers. 'I bet he's got some fantastic stories; can we come and meet him too?'

'We can only ask,' said Mrs Baldwin, before taking a sip of water from her bottle and settling back down with her book.

On their way back to Burty's, they stopped at the police station. Mr Baldwin knocked on the door, but there was no reply. Blue must be out and about, so they continued their journey home.

As they arrived at the last corner before Burty's, it quite amused them to see the Wolfes in the road, in full view of everyone, arguing with Blue about going back to the station. Quite a crowd had gathered as they were making a terrible racket.

'We're not coming with you.'

'You must. I need to ask you some questions.'

'Why, we haven't done anything?'

'It's just routine.'

'But we're on holiday.'

As their voices got louder and the crowd got bigger, Blue finally had enough.

'Do I have to arrest you?'

Suddenly, the brothers fell silent. They realised it was pointless arguing, and they were just drawing more and more unwelcome attention to themselves, so finally they agreed.

'But we don't want those pesky Baldwins hearing anything of this. The last thing we want is this to get back to North Wales. Imagine, the embarrassment of it all.'

As they followed Blue up the road towards the station, a cheery "hello" and a wave from Charlie and Lizzie greeted them.

They snarled at the children as they went past, looking terrifying with their near black eyes.

Chapter 20: Purgatory

'Well, they didn't look happy,' said Lizzie once they were out of earshot, grinning from ear to ear.

'Right, who's coming to Eglit's Emporium?' asked Mrs Baldwin.

'Me,' came the uniform reply.

With a left turn, they headed towards the shop. When they arrived, they saw Vin at the top of a stepladder stacking shelves.

'Welcome, welcome. What can I do for you on this fine day?'

'We came to speak to you, or perhaps your grandfather if he's around, about the history of the island,' said Mrs Baldwin.

'That's more my grandfather's thing. I'll just see whether he is welcoming visitors. He gets quite tired nowadays as the day wears on.'

Vin disappeared out the back. A minute later, he beckoned them through.

'He's sitting in the garden out the back.'

As they walked through the passageway to the garden, they noticed that every inch of wall had shelving on it, with each shelf packed to the brim with goods.

Out in the garden, a smart, casually dressed old man welcomed them. Eglit, as all people do, had shrunk with age, now standing about five feet tall. He was skinny as a rake and spritely for a man of his years, fairly springing out of his chair to greet them.

He had a kind face that sported a natural smile. True, he had grey hair and wrinkles, but his general demeanour was that of a much younger man.

'Please sit,' he said, 'and tell me how I can help you.'

After some brief introductions, Mr Baldwin got to the point of the visit.

'We're really after some background information about the island, something that you don't get from the tourist guides.'

'So, you're after pirates' gold,' he said with a grin on his face. 'Well, they have passed the story down over the years that this is where Calico Jack buried his treasure. People have been looking for it since well before my time, so I wouldn't hold out too much hope of finding anything.'

'Actually, we wanted to ask if anyone on the island practiced voodoo,' interrupted Charlie rather impatiently.

Eglit's eyes lit up. This was obviously a question that didn't come up often.

'Voodoo is on many islands in the Caribbean, and this one is no different.'

'So it is here,' said a rather excited Lizzie.

'Of course, my dear. But like many religions, it is perhaps not as popular as it once was. Shall I go on?'

'Please do,' replied Charlie, fascinated by what he was hearing.

'In the voodoo religion, people like you and I are simply spirits that inhabit the visible world, but there is also an unseen world populated by spirits called the *lwa.* During rituals, the *lwa* can inhabit someone's body and they can then perform incredible physical feats and even cure the sick. When you hear mention of spirits, this is usually what is meant.'

'But the sign on the other sign of the island,' said Lizzie, 'telling people to "stay away", has that got anything to do with voodoo? That's what Burty told us.'

'I think not. Voodoo is not something to be afraid of. That is more the stuff of Hollywood and people's imaginations. It is about restoring balance and energy. Besides, there are other things to worry about on that part of the island.'

The Baldwins were now all absolutely intrigued by what they were hearing.

'When I was a young boy, so about a hundred years ago now, a young girl, a friend of mine, found a brooch covered with rubies and diamonds. Some people imagined it stolen, but she swore she had found it down by Whaler's Bay, or Gravedigger's Bay, as they used to call it. We were sure it was genuine, probably worth a small fortune, so we warned her never to wear it, but our protestations fell on deaf ears. About a week later, just after sunset, we saw her grappling in the street with two men we had never seen before. They grabbed the brooch, throwing her to the ground as they made their escape. The men hadn't spotted us, so as soon as they had gone, we rushed over to check on Lily. She sat there, dazed but fine, so my friend Leon and I followed the two assailants. We followed them at a distance and we finally ended up at

169

the track by the sign you have been talking about. We continued along the path until we came to a small village. It was old, dirty and smelt awful. The men disappeared through a door, so we snuck up and looked through the window. It was a bar, noisy with the sounds of revelry. The two men gave the brooch to a man who, in return, gave them each a drink. We were just about to turn and run when a giant of a man grabbed us both by the scruff of the neck and threw us through the door. We looked up and found ourselves surrounded by what looked like pirates.'

They could see that Eglit was reliving the entire ordeal as he spoke.

'The man with the brooch was obviously in charge, as he was the one who spoke to us and asked us our names. "Well, Leon and Eglit, if you ever breathe a word of what you have seen or heard tonight, not only will you disappear, but your entire families will disappear. You will never be seen, or heard of again". We could see from his face he was being serious. But we were very young and absolutely terrified, so they let us go, confident that their threats would ensure that their secret was safe. But not before one of them had told us the name of the place; "and welcome to Purgatory" he boomed. Neither Leon nor I ever mentioned it again.'

'So, you think they are still there?' asked Charlie.

'I can't say for sure, but this is the first time I have ever told the story to anyone, Vin included. I figure after a hundred years I've got nothing to worry about.'

'What an incredible story,' said Mr Baldwin. 'You've been very helpful. If there is ever anything we can do for you, please let us know, Eglit.'

'It was my pleasure. I am glad to have shared it after all these years. It's a weight off my shoulders. There was a happy ending, by the way. Ten years later, I married Lily.'

With the story concluded, the Baldwin family rose, thanked Eglit for his time, and made their way back through the shop.

'Did my grandfather help you at all?' said Vin, peering down from the top of the stepladder. 'He knows the island and the people like the back of his hand, and his mind is still as sharp as it ever was. If he couldn't help you, I can't imagine who can.'

'He was amazing,' said Charlie. 'I'd love to come back and talk to him some more before our holiday is over.'

'By all means. He'll tell you if he gets tired, so pop round any time. He loves company.'

There was a lot of food for thought, what with voodoo practiced on the island and the fact that there used to be an entire village inhabited by pirates. Anyway, it meant their bags of coins were now doubly safe.

'I wonder how Blue's getting on with Peregrine and Edward Wolfe?' questioned Mr Baldwin as they approached their rooms.

'Guilty as charged,' laughed Mrs Baldwin.

The children weren't so sure. They hadn't seen Catweazle for a couple of days now. There must be a reason for that. If he hadn't taken the gold, surely he would still be close at hand. Then a light clicked on in Charlie's head.

'I've had a thought. If Catweazle was watching our rooms, which I think he probably was, then he'll know who the thieves are. I bet you that's where he is now. That's why we haven't seen him recently.'

'You're right,' said Lizzie. 'Catweazle has to be the key. Either he has the treasure, or he knows who has it. If we can find him, then we'll find what we're looking for.'

'Let's see how Blue got on with the Wolfes first,' said Mr Baldwin. 'I think you might find that we don't need to track down Catweazle at all. Right, who wants a drink?'

After a quick wash and brush up, they left their rooms and made themselves comfortable at the bar in Burty's. Sandra was on duty and brought them over a small bowl of nuts.

'The usual?'

'Yes please, Sandra,' said Mrs Baldwin.

Just as their drinks arrived, the main door swung open. The sight of two seething brothers striding towards them wiped the smiles off their faces.

'I suppose you think that was funny,' one of them said, addressing Mr Baldwin.

'Sorry, I don't understand what you're talking about.'

'You know exactly what I'm talking about. We've just been as good as accused of stealing a chest full of gold coins. We know you're up to something and

172

believe me, we'll find out what, and when we do, you'll be in big trouble.'

With their rant over, the Wolfe brothers turned and marched out of Burty's and back to The Grand.

It wasn't quite what the Baldwins had planned for the start of the evening. The shock of it left them speechless for a minute or two, whilst they processed what they had just witnessed. The brothers had been angry rather than overly aggressive, but what struck them most was what they had said.

'They said they know we're up to something. That's not what you'd say if you had stolen the gold, is it?' said Mr Baldwin. Just as he finished talking, in walked Blue.

'I'm terribly sorry, but as soon as I had finished questioning them, they stormed off, saying that they were going to have a strong word with you. I came as quickly as I could, but I had to lock up the station first.'

'It wasn't a problem,' said Mrs Baldwin. 'I think they talk the talk, but whether they walk the walk is a different matter. Did you find anything out?'

'I need it confirmed, but it looks like they have an alibi. Apparently, at the time in question, they were having breakfast on their terrace. They also said that the gardener was working nearby and can probably confirm that they were there for most of the morning. As for Catweazle, he says he was alone in the woods. Given the way he lives, an alibi will be hard to come by.'

Lizzie smiled. 'I told you Catweazle was the key.'

Blue turned and looked at her questioningly. But he didn't have time to hang about. He needed to find the gardener, so with another apology, he turned and left.

Over dinner, the Baldwins discussed their strategy for the next day. Charlie suggested that he and Lizzie make an early start and head over to Catweazle's. He would still be there if they set off early enough, so they could lie in wait and see what he did. If he stayed put, then he must be the culprit. If he moved off, they would follow him to see if he knew who had the chest and where. They would then come back and update their parents before they all went over to the police station to report it to Blue.

'I don't like the idea of you going near Catweazle's again,' said Mr Baldwin.

'But we won't be going near him or his hut. We promise to keep our distance. We'll choose a vantage point so we can see him clearly from a distance,' said Charlie.

'We can take one of your phones too, just in case,' added Lizzie.

Mrs Baldwin was deep in thought. What would her parents have done if it were her?

'We can go really early so he won't be suspecting anything,' said Charlie. 'He's so used to watching other people, I don't think there's any way he'll be looking out for anyone checking up on him.'

The discussion continued for some time, every argument having a counterargument.

As the other three continued, Mrs Baldwin sat there quietly, looking at her hands holding her coffee. She still had ten fingers AND ten toes, even after what she and her parents had been through in Africa, let alone South America. She had made up her mind.

'OK, you can go, but here are the rules. If you disobey any of them, that's it, trust broken, and it will never, I repeat, never, happen again.'

Her intervention caught the other three by surprise, but she laid out the rules and the children agreed to each and every one.

Charlie and Lizzie were both fast asleep when the alarm on their mother's phone went off. It was still dark outside, although the sun, nearing the horizon, had given the sky a dark orange glow. Charlie got out of bed and gave his sister a good shake.

'Come on Lizzie, it's time.'

Normally this would have been the cause for an argument, but they both knew the importance of their undertaking, so Lizzie obligingly pulled back her covers, rolled to the edge of the bed and got up.

Their mother had put some pieces of fruit out for them, so they popped these in their rucksacks along with a bottle of water each and the essentials. Minutes later, they left the safety of their room, locking the door behind them.

The children walked in silence, too tired to talk. But nothing needed saying. They knew the plan of action. Hurrying through the town and along the path towards Gravedigger's Bay, they listened to the birdsong, which got progressively louder as the sun brought the world back to life.

They left the track and made their way more cautiously through the trees. They had done this many times before, but who was to know what time Catweazle arose? He had strange habits and could just as easily have been out all night.

Once they had spotted the hut, they looked around for the ideal place to settle. The children retreated as far as they could, as per instructions, whilst making sure that they had an excellent view of the surrounding area. They found a small bush, which afforded them enough cover that they could relax and enjoy some breakfast.

'I still think it was the Wolfes,' whispered Charlie. 'I reckon last night was just a great bit of acting. They'd had plenty of time to prepare.'

'And bribe the gardener? But if Catweazle had a friend to help him.'

'I don't think he has any friends.'

The sound of someone humming brought an abrupt end to the conversation. The children sat there, motionless, hearts racing at a hundred miles an hour as it slowly got louder. All their attention had been on the hut. Not for one minute had they thought about looking behind them. Out of the corner of their eyes, they spied Catweazle, not more than ten feet away. He stopped and looked around. The children held their breath.

Chapter 21: Does Catweazle Know?

The seconds felt like an eternity as Catweazle stood there, taking in the vista. He took a large intake of breath, and strode down the slope towards home, and with one last look around, disappeared inside.

It was nearly an hour before Lizzie spotted any action from down at the hut. She nudged Charlie, who was dozing away. They had agreed to take turns keeping lookout; it was still very early, and after the initial excitement, tiredness was getting the better of them.

Catweazle continued with what was no doubt his normal daily routine. This proved more interesting than they expected, as the first thing that he did was clean his teeth; using a twig! He rinsed his mouth out with a handful of water taken from a bucket, grabbed a small bundle, and headed off towards the sea. The children, aware that he might have started his journey, followed. He walked around the excavation site and stripped off completely. Then he walked into the water and started splashing around. The children weren't too shocked. It would have been a quite natural way of washing yourself if you assumed you weren't being watched. On exiting the water, he unravelled the bundle and started drying himself with an old and rather grubby sheet. He returned to the hut, and the children once again continued their vigil from behind the bush.

After a rather meagre breakfast of raw eggs and fruit, which explained how skinny he was, Catweazle entered the hut. He was inside for about ten minutes, with Charlie and Lizzie becoming increasingly frustrated as they couldn't see what he was up to. When he exited, he had a leather water pouch, which he duly filled from the bucket, and a large knife.

Before he left, he had a good look around to check that everything was quiet. Finally, he set off down to the beach, the children tailing him at a safe distance. They were quite comfortable with the way things were going, although it concerned Charlie that they might lose him in the trees if they stayed too far back.

Once at the beach, Catweazle turned left and raced along the sand. At the end of the beach, he climbed up some small rocks. Once on top, he turned and looked back across the bay. The children, trying to remain well hidden, had been following just in the treeline at the edge of the beach. When they saw him turn, they froze.

Catweazle, confident that no one was there, turned back and carried on into the woods. The children hurried along the beach and clambered up the rocks. It wasn't an arduous climb, but they were, for the time being, fully exposed for the world to see.

As soon as they reached the top, they strained their eyes, looking for any sign of him.

'There,' said Lizzie, pointing. 'Come on.'

Catweazle was moving at speed, something made more incredible because he wasn't wearing shoes. To keep up with him, the children were almost jogging, something made hazardous not only by the undergrowth and fear of tripping but also by Catweazle, who would stop randomly and scan around for unwanted company.

They had been racing through the trees for nearly half an hour and were getting quite exhausted. The terrain was undulating, which made the trip even harder. As they progressed, Charlie kept looking around and making a mental note of any distinctive landmarks so they could make their way safely back home. But it was exciting and their adrenalin was pumping, so although it was tiring, they kept up.

As Catweazle approached the brow of the next hill, he slowed down to a crawl. Charlie and Lizzie watched as he stopped completely. He dropped to his knees and lay face down on the ground. He pulled himself up the last yard and peered over, examining what was going on below. The children needed to see what had captured his interest, so they moved in a large arc, maintaining their distance, until they reached a suitable vantage point.

They looked down and didn't really see much at first. Then they noticed movement; movement everywhere. They couldn't believe their eyes. It was exactly as Eglit had told them in his story. There was a village that appeared cut off from the rest of the world. It was difficult to make out at first, as not only was it amongst the trees, but the colour of the buildings helped it merge seamlessly into the surroundings. As they looked closer, they noticed it was a hive of activity, with people busying themselves with their daily chores. There were women clustered around a large flat rock, washing their clothes. Children were carrying buckets of water on wooden poles balanced across their shoulders. Meanwhile, a group of men were preparing nets by their boats, hidden in the trees closest to the sea.

The village was at the back of a small inlet, discretely positioned out of view. The bay itself looked extremely deep judging by the dark blue water, and there wasn't a grain of sand in sight, it being entirely bordered by rocks. It was the perfect hideaway. No beach, too deep to anchor, not much to attract visitors at all.

The boats the men were working on looked as if they were lowered into the sea using a craning system of timber and rope, which lay close by. When they returned, they would winch them out of the water again and hide them from view.

On the slope directly below where they now found themselves, Charlie and Lizzie saw people working in small clearings, covered in greenery.

The children looked at each other in amazement. It was like going back hundreds of years.

Remembering what their mother had said in her lecture about caution at all times, they had seen enough. With one eye on Catweazle and the other on the terrain, they withdrew back down the slope. Finally, out of sight and earshot, they ran as fast as their legs would carry them. They couldn't wait to tell their parents; or Eglit!

In their excitement and throwing caution to the wind, they arrived back at their room in record time. Best thing of all was that because of the preposterously early start, they were back at nine-thirty, so still in time for breakfast. The rooms were empty, so they checked they were both presentable and sped off to the restaurant. To neither of their surprise, they found their parents, heads buried in their books and drinking coffee.

Mrs Baldwin looked up. She couldn't help but feel relieved everything had gone by without incident and the children had returned unscathed. She had her book in her hands, but her mind was elsewhere, as it had been all morning. Charlie and Lizzie hadn't seemed daunted by their task, and her husband's confidence in them had helped her somewhat. But mothers always worry about their children. That's a fact.

'So how did it go?' asked Mr Baldwin.

'It was unbelievable Dad, we found the village that Eglit told us about,' said a very excited Charlie. 'And it's still got people living there, too.'

'How on earth did you find it?' asked their mother.

'We followed Catweazle, just like we said we would, and he led us straight there. We didn't go into the village though, we just watched from a distance, but if our theory about Catweazle is right, the chest is somewhere in Purgatory.'

'And if what Eglit said is true, then I don't expect we stand much chance of getting it back,' said Mr Baldwin.

'Shall we tell Blue?' said Lizzie.

'I can't imagine the inhabitants of Purgatory will worry too much about the police,' said Mrs Baldwin. 'Blue could just end up being one of those folks we never hear of again. We need to give it more thought, because if we make the wrong decision, this could get extremely dangerous. I think there are several questions we must ask ourselves before we do anything.'

'Like what?' asked Lizzie.

'Is the chest definitely there? After all, how did they get to know about it in the first place? The only people who knew about it were us, the Wolfe brothers and potentially, I say that because we still can't be certain, Catweazle.'

This question alone got everyone thinking.

'Charlie still thinks it might be the Wolfes. He thinks they might just have been acting last night to put us off the scent. And they could have paid the gardener to give them an alibi.'

'Perhaps we should wait for some more news from Blue,' said Mrs Baldwin. 'After all, he is on our side and I'm sure he knows what he's doing. As for the gardener, we should let Blue be the judge of whether he's telling the truth. It's a small community, so he should know if he's trustworthy or not.'

The children waved at Sandra and ordered bacon and eggs with the obligatory fried bakes. They were starving.

After breakfast, Charlie and Lizzie suggested they go back to Gravedigger's Bay, as it looked like the excavations were just about over. With no one objecting to the idea, other than a small grumble from Mr Baldwin about the long walk, they set off. They were travelling lighter than normal, as Mrs Baldwin had decided that once they had been for a swim and found out about the burial site, they could head back to town and grab some proper lunch for a change.

As the children had deduced from their earlier excursion, the excavation was complete, and the team were "bagging up" the skeletons for their safe removal and analysis. Once the team had finished this, they said that they would open up the restricted area to the public, but not before raking over the sand. There would be no sign that they had ever been there at all.

'It's rather sad really,' said Charlie. 'It shows how quickly time has flown and how little time we have left before we have to go home.'

For the rest of the morning, Mrs Baldwin ploughed through yet another book and Mr Baldwin sat there silently, not seeing or hearing anything. He, like the children, only had one thing on his mind. Ideas were slowly but surely coming; and they wouldn't have to involve Blue.

'Right,' he said, standing up, 'let's go, there's no time to waste. This holiday won't last forever. We need to get things done. First things first, let's get back and grab some lunch, then I think we need to talk to Eglit. He's a wise man who knows the island and its people better than anyone. I think we might have to let him into our secret if we want to engage his help.'

This took Charlie and Lizzie aback. As much as they liked Eglit, in reality, they had only met him once, so didn't know whether he was truly trustworthy and worth confiding in. Or was their father up to something? Only time would tell.

After a rather nice, but simple lunch in town, the Baldwins made the brief journey back to Burty's. Mr Baldwin, who had drunk two glasses of wine at lunch, said he was feeling rather tired and was going for a snooze. The children, exhausted from their early morning adventure, had no arguments and said they could do with a lie down as well. Mrs Baldwin had just started a new book, so a couple of hours' peace would suit her down to the ground.

At four o'clock, and much to his wife's annoyance, Mr Baldwin's alarm went off. He rolled slowly off the bed and went next door, where he found the children lying there chattering away.

'Any good ideas?' he asked as he stretched and yawned.

'Not really,' Charlie replied. 'We're waiting to see what Eglit says before we put our minds to anything.'

'Me too. I've had a couple of thoughts which I don't think are bad, but I'd like to hear what he has to say about a few things before I have anything more concrete.'

Mrs Baldwin, for her part, hadn't come up with anything. She'd just got another ninety uninterrupted pages under her belt.

After a quick shower, Mr Baldwin suggested they make their way to Eglit's Emporium. As usual, Vin greeted them, this time from the top of a ladder. He was out the front cleaning the windows.

'Good afternoon, lovely people, and how are you all doing today?'

'Very well, thank you, Vin,' replied Mrs Baldwin. 'We need to do some shopping, but we were wondering whether we might have another chat with your grandfather first if that is ok.'

'I'll just check if he's receiving visitors.'

Moments later, Vin returned, asking them to go on through.

'You know the way,' he said, grabbing the rag out of the bucket and continuing with the windows.

Chapter 22:   Time to Think Again

The Baldwins walked through the shop into the garden and Eglit rose from his chair. Judging by his expression, he seemed thrilled to see them again.

'First things first, can I offer you all a cup of tea?'

'That would be lovely,' replied Mrs Baldwin.

Charlie grimaced but bit his lip. He'd tried the tea on his first morning and was still getting over it.

Eglit rose and in no time was back with a big pot of tea and five mugs.

'What can I help you with today?'

Mr Baldwin recounted the story of the children finding the treasure and it being stolen from their room. He also mentioned that the Wolfe brothers and Catweazle were, as far as they were aware, the only people to know about their discovery.

'I knew it existed; I knew it!' squealed Eglit, clenching and shaking his fists in excitement. 'People have hunted for it ever since I can remember. I thought someone had already discovered it and it was long gone. But I never doubted that it existed. Now, Catweazle, he's a funny one. If I remember rightly, he found what he presumed was a piece of pirate treasure when he was very young. It was nothing really, a piece of costume jewellery, but ever since that day, he became obsessed with the legend of Calico Jack and his treasure. The more his obsession took hold, the more reclusive he became, until finally, he felt there wasn't anyone he could trust. I would imagine by now he has searched most places on the island. He lives in a hut in the woods. One thing about Catweazle, though, he keeps his eyes on absolutely everything.'

'Of course you won't have met the Wolfes,' said Mr Baldwin, 'but apparently they've got an alibi as to their whereabouts at the time of the robbery. The gardener from The Grand. You must know him and whether he's trustworthy?'

'What, Gumby? He's not the sharpest tool in the shed, but he's as honest as the day is long. Used to be a sign-writer. Wrote the sign for Betty's Guesthouse,' he said, chuckling to himself. 'He wouldn't lie. It's more a case of whether he would remember. But let me ask you a question now. How did the perpetrator get into your room?'

'They used a spare key that's kept hanging up in the office, the one the cleaner uses,' said Lizzie.

'Would Catweazle or the Wolfes know where they kept it?'

'They'd just need to look around,' said Charlie.

'Don't you think that would have been suspicious? Imagine if someone had spotted them snooping about.'

The entire family suddenly fell silent.

'Perhaps you should try broadening the net. I agree that you've identified the most likely suspects, but something doesn't seem right to me. What about the cleaner? If you had the chest in your room, perhaps they found it by accident and couldn't resist.'

'I don't think we've even seen the cleaner, and we hid the chest under a pile of dirty laundry,' said Charlie.

'That's exactly the sort of thing a cleaner might look for. They could have just thought the pile needed tidying up, and hey presto.'

He had a point. They had all been so focused on Catweazle and The Wolfes that they had given little thought to anyone else. The cleaner made perfect sense, well, as much sense as anyone else. Blue had been more intelligent than they thought when he had said he would start with a comprehensive list and whittle it down one by one. Eglit might have been 110, but he was 110 years wise, not 110 years old.

They finished their tea, which, to Charlie's delight, tasted just as it did back home.

'Thank you ever so much for your hospitality, Eglit,' said Mrs Baldwin.

'Yes, thanks,' said Mr Baldwin. 'It's been great talking to you again.'

'The pleasure has been all mine. If anything else comes to mind, I'll get a message to you via Vin. In the meantime, if there is something you might like to run past me, just pop in. You know where I am.'

The Baldwins walked back through the shop, grabbing a few things on their way, paid and said their goodbyes to Vin.

'Goodbye, my dear people. Thank you so much for coming to visit my grandfather. He's got a new lease of life since he met you.'

'Well, your grandfather's given us a fair bit to mull over,' said Mr Baldwin.

No-one replied. They were all too busy thinking.

By the time they got back, it was early evening. Mr Baldwin suggested they order drinks for the veranda outside their rooms. It would be more private and give them a chance to plan their next move.

Charlie toddled off to find Sandra, who arrived five minutes later with a trayful of drinks.

'I brought you some crisps with some of my home-made dips.'

Mrs Baldwin looked up. The one thing she enjoyed more than reading was eating; and Sandra was proving to be very handy in the kitchen.

'Thank you, Sandra. I'm sure we'll enjoy those.'

Sandra smiled before making her way back to the bar.

'So what are your ideas, Dad?' said Charlie, eager to hear his father's thoughts.

'Now that we've spoken to Eglit, I must admit, I'm rather flummoxed.'

'Lizzie and I have been chatting. Can we all agree on one thing? It wasn't Catweazle. It would have been too heavy for him to lift on his own and as Eglit has confirmed, he doesn't trust anyone, so who would he have got to help him?'

'Let's say we all agree,' replied his father.

'That narrows it down to the Wolfes, someone with access to the room like the cleaner, or someone who overheard us talking and knows the whereabouts of the key.'

'Agreed,' came the uniform reply.

'Do we also agree that Catweazle is the most likely person to have seen who took it and that it is now probably lying in Purgatory?'

'It makes sense,' said Mr Baldwin. 'But if it was the Wolfes, then that wouldn't make sense. They don't even know about Purgatory.'

'Exactly, so we've come up with a plan, one that should kill two birds with one stone. How about setting a little trap for the Wolfes, letting them know where the treasure is? If they've got the chest, they'll ignore it and chuckle to themselves. If not, they'll go looking for it.'

'What, send them to Purgatory?'

'You don't want to go to Purgatory, it could be dangerous,' said Mrs Baldwin, who appeared not to have been listening to a word they said.

The others looked across to see her, apparently engrossed in her book, with a face covered in tiny bits of crisp and dip of all description. Glad she's taking it all so seriously, they thought!

But she was taking it far more seriously than they realised, with her mind racing away with all the various permutations. Whilst they were talking about the chest, she was working out how to keep them all safe, just as her parents had always done for her.

A trip to Purgatory might be dangerous, true, which is why the children had planned on sending the Wolfes there to get the treasure rather than go themselves. It would, after all, be much easier to retrieve once it was back in the town.

'Someone should stay here tomorrow as well, to see who cleans our rooms. We shouldn't forget that's still a possibility,' said Lizzie.

'But if Edward and Peregrine don't have the treasure and it isn't in Purgatory, we will have sent them there for nothing,' said Mr Baldwin.

The children smiled, and Mr Baldwin joined them. None of them noticed the slight upturn in the corners of Mrs Baldwin's mouth, too.

Charlie and Lizzie returned to their room to put the finishing touches to their plan, and with a bit of time to relax, their parents wandered off to find Sandra and order some more drinks and dips.

An hour later, two ravenous children joined them. From the looks on their faces, they seemed very pleased with themselves.

'You haven't booked a table yet, have you?' said Charlie. 'We need to eat at The Grand.'

'If the Wolfes are there,' added Lizzie.

'We hadn't thought that far ahead. Let's finish our drinks, then we'll go,' said Mr Baldwin.

Sure enough, when they arrived at The Grand, there in the far corner of the terrace sat Edward and Peregrine Wolfe. The brothers saw them come in, jumped to their feet, and came over to talk to them. There was nothing the Baldwins could do but stand there, and they soon found themselves overpowered by the pungent aroma of mothballs.

'We are so sorry for our behaviour yesterday evening,' said Edward (or was it Peregrine Wolfe). 'Emotions were running high and we think it best if we could all put this well and truly behind us. Let's not say another word about it.'

'Agreed and apology accepted,' said Mr Baldwin, 'and thank you.'

The brothers nodded their heads politely and returned to their table.

'We must sit on a table quite close by,' said Lizzie once they were out of earshot, 'one they pass on their way out.'

Having found the perfect table, a rather relaxing and uneventful dinner ensued. Her father having settled the bill, Lizzie reached into her pocket and took out a small notebook. She placed it on the table in full view next to her empty glass. Mr Baldwin was about to get up when Charlie put his hand on his father's arm.

'We just need to wait for movement from their table, then we should go.'

It wasn't long before one of the brothers pushed his chair back and stood.

'Now' said Charlie, and the Baldwins got up, gave the Wolfes a wave goodbye, and left.

Peregrine Wolfe was on his way back from the toilet when he glanced across at the Baldwin's table. They had left something behind, a small red notebook. As he passed the table, he looked around to see if anyone was looking and ever so carefully slipped the book into his pocket. On his return to the table, he leant down, whispered in his brother's ear, who promptly wiped his mouth with his napkin, arose, and walked swiftly with his brother back to their room.

As the door clicked shut, Peregrine Wolfe took the notebook from his pocket. His brother at his side, he turned to the first page. It was Lizzie's holiday log. To their great relief, she hadn't written too much and most of it seemed like boring holiday stuff. But then, as they carried on, there it was, jackpot!

It detailed where they had found the treasure and how they had got it back to Betty's Guesthouse. It even mentioned Lizzie dropping the doubloon. Next, of course, came the robbery and Blue's involvement. Then, more by luck than judgement, Lizzie and her brother Charlie had followed Catweazle to its current location, a village completely unknown to the outside world. More to the point, she had explained exactly how to get there!

'The fool,' sneered Peregrine.

Chapter 23:   A Close Shave

'You don't think it a little farfetched that there is a village on the island, a small island like this, that nobody knows about?' said Edward

'If it wasn't there, then why would she write about it? She even says about how to find it?'

'I suppose you're right. Anyway, investigating it won't cost us anything.'

Peregrine noted down the directions and returned to the Baldwin's table. He glanced around to check nobody was watching, then popped the notebook back exactly where he had found it. As he was doing so, Lizzie walked back onto the terrace with Charlie.

'There it is!' she said.

'Are you after this? I had just spotted it and was going to take it to reception. That saves me a job. Here you are.'

'Thank you, Mr Wolfe. Enjoy the rest of your evening.'

The children smiled all the way back to their rooms, where they were met by their two very proud parents.

'Are you sure he had a look at it?' asked their father.

'Certain,' said Charlie, 'we saw him coming back as we got to the door, so waited until he'd put it down. He made up some rubbish story about going to hand it in at reception.'

'Anyway,' said Mrs Baldwin, another book in hand, 'let's all get a good night's rest. It looks like we might be quite busy tomorrow and we must make another early start.'

They all adjourned for bed, and in no time, all fell silent.

The discussion over breakfast revolved around who should do what. They decided that two of them would stay at the guesthouse and watch out for the cleaner, whilst the other two monitored the Wolfes. The brothers had taken the bait hook, line and sinker, so it was just a question of whether it was them who had the treasure or they knew it to be somewhere else. Either way, by the end of the day, the Baldwin family would know a lot more.

Then the talk turned to the pairings. The children were keen to keep in the same groups as before, and for once, their parents had no genuine disagreement. After all, said their mother, they had followed Catweazle to Purgatory successfully, so this should be a much easier proposition. But the same strict set of rules applied. Safety was, as always, paramount.

Mr and Mrs Baldwin gathered a few things for their bag. They didn't need much, they weren't going far. Mrs Baldwin proudly announced that all she needed was shade, so a parasol, something to sit on, and her latest book. And some nibbles perhaps, oh yes, and a drink. And I know who will be told to carry all that lot, thought Mr Baldwin.

The children, who were both now becoming quite intrepid and experienced adventurers, knew exactly what they were taking; the essentials and a bottle of water each. Their grandfather, Toe, would have been proud, thought Charlie.

They moved off, going their separate ways. Mr and Mrs Baldwin didn't even need to be too secretive. All they really had to do was vacate the room and then wait for the unsuspecting cleaner. They crossed to the edge of Burty's garden, put the parasol up and the towels down and waited; Mrs Baldwin with her head deep in her book in seconds. Her husband was there, keeping an eye out, so all was well.

As for Charlie and Lizzie, they were going to have to stay out of sight. A genuine sense of excitement filled the air as they hunted around for a decent vantage point. Today was going to be the day when they found out if the Wolfes were innocent or guilty.

They settled for a spot some distance away from The Grand, obscured by an old and rather dirty parked car. Raised flower beds bordered the side of the road, and the children sat on the low retaining wall and waited.

'They might have gone already,' said Lizzie in a mild panic.

'It's still pretty early. I'd be surprised.'

'Should one of us go to the hotel and see if we can spot them?'

'That'd be too dangerous, Lizzie. If they don't come out in the next half an hour, I've got another idea. I'll nip back to Burty's and ask Sandra if I can use the phone. I'll call The Grand and ask for them and see if they come to the phone.'

As soon as Charlie had finished speaking, two vulture shaped creatures emerged from the front entrance.

'They look like they're off to a funeral,' said Lizzie.

'They always do. Let's hope it's not their own,' Charlie said in jest.

'Shall we tell Mum and Dad, or shall we follow them some of the way, just to check they're going where we think?'

'We should definitely follow them, for a while at least. They might just be going to talk to Blue. Who knows?'

As soon as the Wolfes were out of sight, Charlie and Lizzie ran to the corner of the road. Lizzie peered round. The brothers were sauntering along, deep in conversation.

'I wish they'd move more quickly. We haven't got all day.'

But the children remained not only patient but also alert, something which served them well, as the Wolfes regularly stopped, scanning around to check there was no-one nearby.

After the best part of an hour, one of the brothers pointed his finger. He had seen the sign. They picked up the pace, climbed under the rope and started up the rather indistinct path. Charlie and Lizzie needed to get closer now, as the vegetation was getting thicker, so they hurried to catch up.

The children heard a lot of moaning and groaning from the Wolfes' direction. It would appear that the brothers had discovered why wearing appropriate clothes and footwear might be beneficial.

'They're making quite a lot of noise,' whispered Lizzie. 'Don't you think they'll attract some unwanted attention? Perhaps we should get back.'

'Let's carry on a little longer. It might help if we know exactly where the village is from here, just in case we need to come back.'

It might have been down to the fact that they were such scary characters themselves, but the Wolfes seemed to be oblivious to any danger. That was until they took one step too far. Suddenly, the ground beneath them gave way, and they fell into a pit. It must have been deep, as the children lost sight of them entirely. As they fell, a small rope tied to the trap tightened. The rope was attached, via various pulleys, to a pin in the adjacent tree. The immediate force pulled the pin out, releasing a large hammer that crashed into the side of an old ship's bell. There was an enormous and resounding "DONG", which momentarily drowned out the noise of the brothers in the pit.

Charlie had seen enough. 'Let's go; and stay close.'

Rather than dash back down the path where they would be in plain view, Charlie took them down a parallel route. They moved carefully, but fast, only stopping when they heard some activity behind them.

'What have we here, then?' boomed a voice.

The children, staying absolutely motionless, watched as half a dozen rather burly men dragged the squirming brothers from the pit. Gagging them

198

immediately, amidst rather feeble protestations, they then bound their hands together behind their backs.

'Me and Jim'll take 'em back. The rest of you landlubbing pirates check the woods for any more of 'em,' ordered the man with the booming voice.

It was now or never. Charlie grabbed Lizzie by the arm and ran as fast as he could, younger sister in tow, through the undergrowth. Not once did they look back, but if they had, they would have seen the men slowly working their way down the path, so with every second, they were a step further from danger.

A couple of minutes later, they crossed the road and started down towards Fisherman's Cove. There would be more people there, so they should definitely be safe.

They finally arrived at the road bordering the beach, and to their sheer joy, spotted Tallboy dropping a family off some fifty yards away.

'Have a great holiday, and mind the sharks,' said Tallboy, as the family headed onto the beach.

'That's what you said to us,' said Lizzie, panting away.

'Ah, the skeleton finders! How are you doing?'

'Great thanks, Tallboy,' replied Charlie. 'Any chance of a lift back to Betty's? We can pay you when we get back, our parents are there waiting for us?'

'Sure, it's on my way anyhow. Hop in.'

Charlie and Lizzie jumped in and looked out the back window. With nothing in sight, they heaved huge sighs of relief, and Tallboy pulled away, very slowly!

While the children had been away, Mrs Baldwin had read another fifty pages and somehow eaten all the nibbles herself, something she vehemently denied when her husband asked her where they had all gone. It was late morning when the cleaner finally arrived, and as soon as she was in the room, Mr Baldwin tapped his wife's leg.

'Right, let's go.'

They both hurried to their room, sneaking a peek through the open doorway to see her in operation.

'I won't be long,' said Sandra, instinctively looking up at them. 'When people are staying, I try to keep the rooms exactly as they left them, but cleaner.'

'What about laundry?' asked Mrs Baldwin. 'I read we should pop it in a laundry bag and leave it outside the door, but do you ever check around the rooms to see if anything needs doing?'

'No, we only take the bags. It's much simpler that way and avoids any confusion. Why? Do you need some washing done?'

As relaxed as ever, they could see by her demeanour there was no way she knew anything about what had gone on.

'No thank you, not for the moment, anyway. Is it just you who cleans the rooms?'

'Just me, unless I'm on holiday, which Burty complains about bitterly.'

'He's very lucky to have you. Anyway, we should leave you to it. Have a lovely day, Sandra.'

'You too.'

They turned to get back to their relaxing morning under the parasol, and had only gone a few paces when they spotted Charlie and Lizzie running towards them from the reception area.

'Can we have some money to pay Tallboy? It's a long story,' said Charlie.

'And the magic word?' asked his mother, smiling.

'Please,' said Charlie, rather impatiently.

'I'll pay him. It looks like you need a drink,' said Mr Baldwin, reaching into his wallet and pulling out a twenty-dollar note and handing it to Charlie. 'And don't forget the change.'

Whilst Mr Baldwin was off paying Tallboy, Charlie and Lizzie went and asked Sandra, who they spotted through the open door of their room, whether they could have a couple of bottles of lemonade.

A few minutes later, drinks in hand, the children joined their parents in the garden.

'Well, it wasn't the cleaner,' said Mr Baldwin. He stopped there, as he could see that the children were desperate to recount what they had seen.

They were both so eager to get everything out that Mrs Baldwin had to interrupt them more than once and ask them to slow down, but she and her husband sat there, mesmerised by what they were hearing. Once finished, the children looked at their parents to see what they thought. But their faces, looking wide-eyed at Charlie and Lizzie in astonishment, said it all. Eventually, it was Mrs Baldwin who broke the silence.

'Well, I think you put yourselves in a lot of unnecessary danger.'

'Do you think they'll escape?' said Lizzie.

'I think we should have a chat with Eglit sooner rather than later. Who's coming?'

Everyone was standing in an instant.

Chapter 24:   The Party Begins

A few minutes later, they entered Eglit's Emporium. Before they uttered a word, Vin asked them to go straight on through.

Eglit was sitting at the garden table. In front of him was a large teapot with five cups and saucers. He positively leapt from his chair to greet them.

'I'll put the kettle on.'

A few minutes later, once they had all settled down, the children recounted their story to Eglit. He sat there entranced, but emotionless, and it was almost as if he had been expecting the ending when it finally came.

'You've actually been there,' said Mr Baldwin. 'Have you any advice? Should we tell Blue?'

'I would leave the police officer out of this if you can. He has no power in Purgatory, he'll just be another man to them. I am sure the brothers will be safe for the time being, in the long term who knows, but for now they'll be ok, if perhaps a little less comfortable than usual.'

The children looked at their mother. Her face gave little away, as always, but they could tell she didn't like the situation.

'I suppose it was us that got them into this situation, so it should be us that gets them out of it,' she suddenly piped up.

'And how do you propose to do that?' asked Eglit. 'You mustn't forget, these are people who live outside the bounds of the law as we know it, so "normal" won't apply. They'll have a code or rules which they live by, and I would imagine that you might have breached those already.'

'But we must do something.'

'If you insist, which I imagine is the brave thing rather than the wise thing to do. But you'll need a plan, a good plan. You won't be able to accomplish much before nightfall, anyway. Why don't we all think about it over lunch and meet back here mid afternoon before moving off? One more thing, I'm going to tell Vin if that is ok with you? He's like a second son to me and you can trust him with anything.'

'Please do whatever you think is best.'

They said their farewells until the afternoon and were off.

'I'm glad we spoke to him,' said Charlie.

Everyone nodded in agreement.

They talked about every potential outcome over lunch, but they all came to the same conclusion: they'd just have to wait until they got there. Nobody really knew what they were up against, not even Eglit. After all, a lot must have changed in 100 years, including the people. They needed to prepare for every eventuality, which would require some thought, as there was only so much they could take with them.

'Do you need some help?' asked Lizzie.

'With what?' said her father.

'What you need to take.'

'What are you taking, children?' interrupted Mrs Baldwin, desperately trying to save her husband from any potential embarrassment.

'The principal thing is the right clothing Mum,' said Charlie. 'If it's night and you haven't got long trousers and long sleeves, you might well get some painful scratches. And mosquito bites, of course. You'll also need some good shoes as we don't know the terrain yet; some of it, yes, but not the last part.'

'And the essentials,' chirped in Lizzie. 'And some water to keep hydrated.' She was quite enjoying being an expert.

'Don't worry about the essentials. We've got those,' said Charlie. But a torch would be handy. Have you got one, Dad?'

'Yes, I'm good thanks Charlie, I brought my old diving torch with me.'

'Grab the foldable spade too, Lizzie. If Eglit doesn't think we need it, we can leave it at his place.'

As Lizzie grabbed the spade, Mr and Mrs Baldwin glanced at each other and smiled. Were these their children they were listening to and watching, going about the entire operation with what they could only describe as military precision?

With everything in the rucksacks, they raced off in search of Eglit. It was time for action.

When they reached Eglit's Emporium, it surprised them to see a sign saying that it was closed for the day. They tried the door. Vin must have locked it. There was a bell midway up the door on the left-hand side, so Charlie rang it and they stood there waiting. This wasn't what they had imagined at all.

Just as they were about to turn and go, Lizzie saw some movement by the back door of the shop and knocked on the glass. A smiling Vin came to the door.

'Sorry about that. We've been so busy getting ready. I had to shut the shop up and I completely forgot that the doorbell needs a new battery. You haven't been waiting long, I hope.'

'WE'VE been getting ready?' questioned Mr Baldwin.

'Oh yes, I haven't seen my grandfather like this in years. Each time you visit, he's like a new man. He's told me the story, by the way. I can't believe it, and I've been living here all of my life!'

'But how's your grandfather going to get there?' said Lizzie. 'It's a long way just to the sign.'

'Don't you worry, young lady; we've been sorting things out ever since you left, and we think we have everything. Now, children, he has a couple of bags in the back garden. Can you get them and tell him we're ready to go? We can discuss the plan of action on the way.'

Charlie and Lizzie popped through to the garden, where a grinning Eglit was eagerly awaiting their return.

'There are the bags,' he said, pointing down by his side. 'Grab one each and let's make a move.'

One bag was enormous, the other a small holdall. The children looked at each other momentarily. There was a minor rush as both children lunged for the

206

holdall, but Charlie had been too quick off the mark for Lizzie and held it aloft in triumph. Lizzie grabbed the other bag, which was mercifully light, and followed Charlie back through the shop. Although it wasn't heavy, the sheer size of Lizzie's bag meant she needed all her concentration to avoid knocking things off the shelves as she moved along. Finally came Eglit, locking the back door behind him.

Once everyone was outside the shop, Eglit asked Lizzie to open the bag and, to her surprise, it was full of cushions. Eglit grabbed them one by one, placing them carefully in a shopping trolley, before asking Vin for a leg up. Rather than a leg up, Vin grabbed him behind his knees and back and lifted him into the trolley.

'Right, let's go,' said Eglit.

They moved off, Eglit grinning from ear to ear. It really did look rather funny, thought the children, Vin pushing Eglit down the road in a trolley.

'Do one of you children want to push?' asked Eglit.

Lizzie took over from Vin without hesitation.

'Come on then, faster, faster!'

Lizzie got up to a jog. Eglit was having a whale of a time.

'Come on faster, I say, now jump on.'

With one last shove, Lizzie jumped on the back, and the two of them went spinning down the road, screaming and laughing.

'Elizabeth,' said Mrs Baldwin sternly, 'stop mucking about. We don't need any accidents before we even get there.'

Lizzie stopped at once. She knew what the use of her full name meant.

'Spoilsport,' said Eglit under his breath.

With no definitive plan, the discussion turned to what they would do given any set of circumstances. It seemed like the best thing to do. Nobody knew quite what lay ahead, so they had to prepare for everything. Vin made it clear that he was going to stay with his grandfather, so it was up to the Baldwins how they wanted to progress as a family.

Once again, the children were quite insistent that they wanted to stay together. After all, why break up a winning team? Eglit, who had calmed down by now and was more than a little exhausted after his initial exertions, had doubts.

'It might get more dangerous from here. You should listen to your parents on this one.'

Mr Baldwin was thinking hard and had a hundred questions going through his head. Who would be the hardest to catch? Who would be the most difficult to spot? Who knew the island better? Who had seen Purgatory before? All these questions and more, and each time he came up with the same answer.

'If your mother agrees, you can stick together, and when I say together, I mean together. You look after your younger sister, Charlie.'

Charlie and Lizzie smiled at each other. Dad always did like a party, and he wasn't going to spoil this one for the children for no reason.

Mrs Baldwin said nothing. She had already been hoping her husband would say exactly that. One thing she didn't want was Charlie or Lizzie anywhere near the village. She would go down with her husband and leave the children with Eglit and Vin in relative safety, not that they would know that, of course.

After much discussion, they agreed on a plan. They would all travel together as far as the trap that the Wolfes had fallen into and would split up thereafter. Mr and Mrs Baldwin would go in first, with the other teams keeping a lookout from separate vantage points, so if captured, one team still had a chance. They would have forty-five minutes in which to do a recce and try to find out where the Wolfes were being held. If, after that time, they hadn't returned, then Charlie and Lizzie would go in. If, after another forty-five minutes, they hadn't come back either, then Eglit and Vin said they had something up their sleeves and would take it from there, although they wouldn't let on what it was, no matter how hard the children pressed them.

'Probably so we don't spill the beans when we're tortured,' joked Charlie.

No-one laughed.

Mrs Baldwin walked in silence, with only one thing on her mind. She and her husband had 45 minutes not only to find the Wolfes, but to keep the children out of harm's way.

Everyone took turns pushing Eglit and the entire trip didn't take long at all, meaning that they reached the sign well before sundown.

'We should wait at least until the light dims,' said Eglit. 'If they have lights in the village, then it'll make it much easier for us to see them than it will them to see us.'

'Don't you think it would be worth making a start?' said Charlie. 'The ground's rather uneven in places, so it will be easier to navigate before the sun goes down. Anyway, won't we be easy to spot later because we'll be using torches to light the way?'

'The moonlight should be enough once our eyes have adjusted, but perhaps we should make a start. Now let's all remember, they could be anywhere. I'm sure they're not too worried about search-parties yet, which is something in our favour, but we should keep absolutely silent once we enter their territory and communicate only with hand signals.'

They all agreed, and Vin extracted his grandfather from the shopping trolley. Once out, Eglit had a good stretch and opened the holdall. It was hard to see exactly what was inside, but he took the first item out, which looked like a modified rucksack with sizeable holes in it. He zipped the bag back up and handed the rucksack to Vin, who slung it over his shoulders and fastened the buckle around his waist.

'Right,' said Eglit, 'it'll be best if we get to the other side of the rope before I hop in.'

He and Vin ducked under the rope, and Vin knelt on the ground. Eglit unzipped the rucksack and turned, so they were back to back. He climbed in, putting one leg in one hole and one in the other. Finally, he zipped himself securely in.

'Come on Vin, let's go.'

Vin got to his feet, his grandfather looking hilarious behind him, with his legs dangling beneath the rucksack.

'Can you pass me the bag, please?' asked Vin, and Lizzie duly obliged. 'I'm glad you've lost weight as you've got older grandfather; I probably couldn't have done this twenty years ago.'

It really was the strangest thing imaginable, a 70-year-old, about to walk up a track, carrying his 110-year-old grandfather on his back, saying he couldn't have done it 20 years ago. No-one was EVER going to believe them now, thought Charlie.

As they walked up the track, there was light enough for Mr Baldwin to give a casual glance to see if there had been any disturbance on the ground anywhere near where he and his wife had hidden their bags. Thankfully, it looked like nothing had changed, and he breathed a sigh of relief.

It wasn't a steep incline, but just steep enough to make them have to stop every few minutes to catch their breath. Progress was slow, mainly because Vin, although not struggling, was taking things very much at his own, very Caribbean, pace.

When they finally got to the part of the track where the Wolfes had been captured, Charlie held up his hand, signalling for all to stop. He had done this some distance from the pit, as he didn't want to make any mistakes at this stage of the game. He pointed to his right, and the entire expedition force moved away from the track and into the woods. This was where the children had watched the men binding the Wolfes before they took them away.

It didn't seem like they had been there that long before the sun dropped beneath the horizon and night fell. Eglit made the signal for them to split up. He pointed at Mr and Mrs Baldwin, then pointed in a direction parallel to the track in the village's direction. Mr Baldwin gave him the thumbs up. Next, Eglit pointed at the children and then the ground by their feet; stay here. Charlie and Lizzie gave him the thumbs up. Finally, he tapped Vin on the shoulder and pointed to the other side of the track. Vin gave him the thumbs up. With a last smile and a nod, the parties went their separate ways.

Chapter 25: Welcome to Purgatory

Mr Baldwin led the way towards the village, making sure at every turn that his wife was still directly behind him. It was a clear night and the moon, although not quite full, lit the surroundings sufficiently well. They hadn't used their torches all evening, so their eyes had adjusted well to the dark and progress was quick. But the ground was still hard to make out in places, particularly where shaded from the moonlight, so the journey involved more than the occasional stumble.

They were now well and truly on their own, having left the rest of the group some distance back, but this gave them a sense of freedom and agility that they hadn't had before. As they continued towards the village, they noticed voices way in the distance. It was a still evening, but now and then, a small gust brought the sound of conversation to their ears. A small path leading from the village to the top of the hill facilitated their progress. It was pretty worn underfoot, which made Mr Baldwin think it must be in regular use. This, along with it not leading to the outside world, made him confident that there wouldn't be any pits to fall into.

He turned, beckoning his wife closer, before grasping her hand as they made their way down the narrow path. Then, in one fell swoop, something swept them clean off their feet, elevating them high in the air. A net, with the stench of fish permeating every

213

fibre, held them in a tight ball. The trap, as the one the Wolfe's had fallen into, had a mechanism to alert the village, and with a loud clang, they knew the clock was ticking.

The sound from the village had instantly become more frantic as people gathered in the street. Mr Baldwin, glad he had ignored what Charlie had said regarding taking the essentials, wriggled around.in the netting. This proved more difficult than he imagined, as it was not only his body that was being contorted into a ball, but also that of his wife. She had unfortunately ended up on top of and somehow entwined with him. He shuffled a bit more. He needed to get his hand into his pocket to retrieve the penknife. Getting things out of your pocket can be incredibly difficult when seated, but trying to get them out when your knees are up by your chin and your wife is on top of you is nigh on impossible. But he continued undeterred, his fear driving him on, until somehow, he managed. Now came the arduous task of getting the blade out. This would have been much easier had he had the use of both hands, but this wasn't the case, so with his right hand, he felt for the groove in top of the blade. Then something whacked him hard in the side.

'And what have we here then?' said a booming voice.

The villagers lowered them to the ground, disentangled them from the netting and pulled them to their feet, rather roughly to Mrs Baldwin's mind. Then they tied their hands behind their backs. The ropes were tight, making it very uncomfortable.

'Can you please just loosen…'

'No speaking unless spoken to,' the man boomed.

It relieved Mrs Baldwin that Charlie and Lizzie weren't with them. It wasn't a pleasant experience being pushed and pulled down the track, and she was glad that she was wearing good shoes. Perhaps they had all underestimated how tough the pirates were, other than Eglit, that was. She now questioned whether their plan had been such a good one, after all. Perhaps it would have been best to leave it all to Blue.

After a couple of minutes, they arrived at the village. Had they been visiting as tourists, it would have seemed quite quaint. The first thing that struck them was the darkness. Although a certain amount of light emanated from almost every window, there was nothing on the street. Eglit had mentioned the appalling smell, but it wasn't nearly as bad as they had imagined. As for the buildings, they were all very simple single-storey structures, with solid wooden walls and natural roofs made from palm leaves collected from the woods.

The Baldwins had little time for sightseeing. As for the villagers, it appeared as if everyone had come outside to see the new arrivals being hustled and bustled down the street. But there was no great animosity, more curiosity than anything else.

Finally, they came to a small, windowless building. A large piece of oak spanned the door, keeping it firmly shut. A short, stocky man stepped forward, lifting it clear, and the door swung open.

As their captors untied them, a surge of blood filled the Baldwins' hands. But their relief was short-lived, as someone shoved them through the door with such force that they only just stayed on their feet.

'Make yourselves comfortable,' said the man with the booming voice, 'whilst the cap'n decides what to do with you.'

He slammed the door shut before replacing the oak with a resounding thud. It was pitch black, and Mrs Baldwin put her arm through her husbands.

'What do we do now?' she whispered.

'Wait for the children, I suppose, but having just seen what they'll be up against, I don't know.' There seemed to be an air of resignation and hopelessness in the reply.

'They're quite clever little things, so let's wait and see,' came the voice of Peregrine (or was it Edward) Wolfe from the other side of the room.

As the forty-five minutes wore on, the children became increasingly nervous. It wasn't so much that they feared for their own safety, but more so for their parents. In their own minds, they had never even contemplated failure, so their parents not returning with something to report now filled them with dread.

With Charlie feeling the vibration of the alarm in his pocket, he knew their time was up. He gave his sister a small tap on the shoulder. Lizzie replied with a thumbs up, and they were off.

Although they realised their parents might just have been slower than expected, the children didn't want to chance taking the same route. They kept well off the beaten track, skirting around the village, at a distance, in an anticlockwise direction. They crossed a couple of paths but resisted the temptation of a straightforward journey in favour of a safer one. As and when they found a little shortcut, they took it, but only when it looked natural rather than artificial or worn by regular use.

Finally, they reached the village, but now came the question of where on earth their parents might be. The village streets, being so poorly lit, made it easy to navigate undetected as they could remain in the shadows. The village was small, but like a maze, with lots of short streets criss-crossing at irregular intervals, meaning that at no point could you see from one end to the other. It would have been easy to get lost had it not been for its relatively small size, but it would still take some thought if they needed to make a quick escape.

As they neared the centre of the village, they heard muffled voices close by. They poked their heads around the corner. The noise was coming from a large building set apart from the others. There was a sign outside, gently swaying back and forth, but it was dark, so impossible to read. Charlie held his index finger up to his lips, then pointed to the open window of the building. As quiet as church mice, they swept across the road and, hugging the edge of the building, made their way to the window. They daren't look in for fear of being seen, so they crouched beneath the window and listened. The low hum of voices emanating from the building indicated a packed room.

Hopefully, the entire village, thought Charlie. Given the number of people, it sounded an orderly discussion.

'That makes four, and there might be more to come.'

'Four in a hundred years. Is it really that bad?'

'But look at them, what they're wearing, they're not from here, they might not frighten that easily.'

'They're not from here, they're from Wales.'

Charlie and Lizzie couldn't believe their ears. Mustering every ounce of courage, they slowly lifted their heads and peered through the window. There he stood, bold as brass. Burty!

They ducked down and looked at each other, eyes and mouths wide open. They now knew how someone had got into their rooms without being noticed.

Charlie pointed down the street, and they retreated until they were out of earshot.

'I can't believe it,' whispered Charlie. 'Burty, of all people. Anyway, it looks like everyone's at the meeting, so let's pray it takes time so we can have a good look around. Make sure you stay close, Lizzie; and not a sound.'

They started looking for a door that showed any sign of being locked. There would be no need for such things in a place like this, so anything that looked secured would need investigating.

Luck was on their side, and it wasn't long before the children came across a door locked from the outside. Ever so delicately, Lizzie withdrew the bolt.

218

As she opened the door, a nanny goat and her kid barged past into the street, bleating as they ran.

As scary as the situation had become, the children had to continue; this was their parents they were talking about. They ran as fast as their legs would carry them away from the immediate vicinity of the goats, before resuming their search. A minute later, they found a door held shut by a large oak beam. With one of them at each end, the children lifted it and lay it on the ground. They opened the door more carefully this time, their mother's cry of joy signalling that their search was over.

'About time,' said Peregrine (or was it Edward) Wolfe.

The children, chuffed to bits, stood there motionless. That was until they both received rather hefty shoves in the back, landing them in a heap on the floor.

'Gotcha,' boomed a voice.

As the door closed behind them, everything went pitch black.

'You children ok?' asked their father.

'Fine thanks Dad, and you?'

'We're good thanks, Charlie.'

'We're fine too,' came a voice as the children noticed the rather powerful aroma of mothballs.

'It was Burty,' blurted out Lizzie. 'He's one of them.'

'Are you sure?' asked Mrs Baldwin.

'We saw him,' said Charlie.

'It makes sense when you think about it,' said Mr Baldwin. 'He knew we were off to find Blue because I asked him for directions. He probably just went for a snoop around our rooms and hit the jackpot.'

'The worst thing is that they're still thinking about what to do with us,' Charlie continued. 'Apparently, this doesn't happen often.'

'This is all your fault,' came the accusing voice of one of the Wolfes.

'Well, we can't just sit here and accept whatever they might have in store for us. Come on, Charlie,' said Lizzie.

That's my girl, thought Mrs Baldwin to herself.

Lizzie switched on her torch, and Charlie did the same. The room was very bleak and there were no windows or doors other than the one they had all entered through. They shone their torches up at the roof, which comprised wooden beams with palm leaves laid across them. There was another click as Mr Baldwin turned on his diving torch, which seemed to be about five times as bright as the other two.

'Make sure you don't shine that in anyone's eyes, Dad, you'll blind them,' said Charlie.

With the room now fully lit, everyone stood and looked around for anything that might provide even the smallest hope of escape. Lizzie saw a dark patch on the roof and asked her father for a shoulder ride. With her father duly obliging, Lizzie gave it a poke.

'It's really soft. Can you pass me your penknife, Charlie?'

220

'And the magic word,' said Charlie, trying to lighten the atmosphere as he passed it across.

Lizzie ignored her brother, opened the saw attachment, and started cutting through the palm leaves. Mr Baldwin wasn't too happy; he was finding it hard not to inhale all the little bits of dust that were falling down with the larger pieces of debris. Within minutes, there was a large enough hole for Lizzie to push her entire hand through.

'There we are,' she said. 'That's a start. Your turn, Charlie. It's quite tiring and working above your head really makes your arm ache.'

Charlie looked at his father as he set Lizzie down. Mr Baldwin, exhausted, smiled back at him, shaking his head.

'I'll do it,' said one of the brothers, dropping to his knees. 'We are a team now, after all.'

While it suits you, everyone thought.

As Charlie climbed aboard, he couldn't help but wonder, even with everything else going on in his mind, how on earth he would get the dreadful odour of mothballs out of his trousers.

The hardest part of the operation had been getting the initial breakthrough, so Charlie made quick work of enlarging the hole. 'It only has to be big enough to push Lizzie through, then she can jump down and open the door for the rest of us.'

'Clever boy,' said the Wolfe brother, forming the other half of the double act.

It hadn't taken long at all, and with Mr Baldwin and Lizzie re-energised, Charlie clambered down.

'Once you're up there, stand up using my head to steady yourself, then try to pull yourself through,' said Mr Baldwin.

With Charlie's help, Lizzie manoeuvred herself so she was kneeling on her father's shoulders. She held tight to his head and eased herself onto her feet. As soon as she was steady, she put one hand on the edge of the hole, then the other. In one swift movement, she put her arms together above her head as if she were about to dive into a swimming pool, and burst through the hole. It was tight, and with Lizzie only halfway out, Mr Baldwin and one of the Wolfes grabbed a foot each and pushed as hard as they could. There was a sudden release of pressure as Lizzie shot out onto the roof.

Chapter 26:   The Voodoo Priest

Lizzie looked around to check it was all clear, and rolled down the sloping roof, stopping at the edge. It was only a small jump down to the ground, which she did without hesitation. The doorway was round the other side of the building, so Lizzie crept along the wall, checking at all times for signs of company. As she peered around the corner, her eyes widened. A sizeable crowd, all holding flaming torches, was approaching fast. I need Eglit, she thought, and ran.

The occupants were all very excited at the sound of the oak beam being lifted from outside the door.

'Well done!' said Mrs Baldwin, whose face immediately dropped when confronted by the rowdy crowd, all sense of hope gone.

'Right, get 'em out.'

'There's only five of 'em Cap'n.'

The cap'n pushed the man aside, grabbing a torch as he strode into the room. He held the torch high to see if anyone was hiding amongst the beams and spotted the hole.

'One of 'em has escaped; find 'em men.'

Half the crowd dispersed immediately, all going in different directions.

'If you touch a hair or her head, I'll…'

'You'll do what?' said the cap'n, staring at Mrs Baldwin, who glared back, unafraid.

'Right, tie 'em up and bring 'em to the tavern.'

They tied the five remaining prisoners up, hands behind their backs, and led them to the principal building in the centre of the village. The tavern looked like it came straight out of an old black and white movie, complete with swinging sign outside denoting its name, "The Hangman's Noose".

As they entered, the first thing that hit them was the smell of stale beer. Simply furnished, it contained some very basic wooden tables and chairs. By the right-hand wall there was a far grander chair with a very elaborate carving depicting various sea battles on the back. Straight ahead there was a long bar, and behind the bar, hanging on the wall, was a rather old and ominous looking noose. And there, in the far-right-hand corner of the room, stood the chest, their chest!

Lizzie, knowing she needed to be out of the village and in the safety of the trees, ran for her life. Remembering the offset of the streets on her way in, she alternated right and then left until she came to the perimeter. With a scan of the horizon and looking at the position of the moon, Lizzie knew the rough direction they originally came from. Thankfully, she wasn't far from where she needed to go into the woods, but erring on the side of caution, she entered where she was and made her way diagonally across. Unlike before, speed was of the essence, as she didn't know how far they were behind her. She ran like the wind, keeping a trained eye out for what lay underfoot as best she could. Although not moving silently, she reckoned that with every yard she put between herself and the villagers, she was one step nearer safety. With any luck, she should have a decent head start if they checked for her in the village first.

Her heart pounding with the exertion, Lizzie stopped and looked back. She could hear activity in the village, but no-one had ventured beyond and into the woods. This meant that she could move more calmly and put more thought into where Vin and Eglit might have gone. She was sure that they must be close by, but there was little way of knowing their exact location.

Suddenly, the village erupted with noise. Lizzie's heart sank as she turned. There were people with torches spilling into the woods in a long line. They seemed close enough together and co-ordinated enough to be carrying out a thorough search. They were concentrating on two areas, highlighting where any exit routes might be. Unfortunately for Lizzie, she was in the middle of one of the search areas, and although they were still some distance away, a terrifying feeling made her feel sick to the core.

Progress was now somewhat slower, as it was imperative she not make a sound whilst keeping out of sight. Now and then she would happen upon a sparsely vegetated area, making her continued concealment even more difficult. Because of the slower pace, the gap was reducing significantly, until Lizzie realised that hiding was her only option. A large rock to her left was a possibility, but she also thought of climbing high in a tree. She turned for one last glance at her tormentors, who were closing in fast. A hand came from behind, covered her mouth, and pulled her down behind the rock.

Vin held a single finger to his mouth. He pointed first at Lizzie and then to the ground.

Eglit stood up and, with Vin's help, clambered on top of the rock. Then Vin fiddled around in the bag at his feet. He lit a couple of smoke bombs and lobbed them to the far side of the rock towards the approaching mob, who Eglit was now facing.

As the torches neared, they illuminated a cloud of purple and red smoke, which slowly cleared to reveal a small, scrawny man standing there on top of a rock. Dressed entirely in black, he was wearing a top hat with colourful beads around his neck. And on his blackened face was a white painted skull. Eglit stood there motionless as more and more people gathered to see what on earth was going on. Each time the smoke thinned, Vin lit another smoke bomb to maintain the feeling of magic and mystery. One thing was certain, Eglit had his audience mesmerised. You could hear a pin drop when he finally spoke; in a slow, beautifully rich voice.

'You, you people of Purgatory, this is not for you to deal with, this is for me. She is in my world now. Go, go back to your homes, unless you want to suffer the same fate as the girl.'

Vin threw one last can of black smoke and a couple of enormous bangers. A mild panic ensued as they exploded, and when the smoke dissipated, there was absolutely no-one in sight.

Lizzie couldn't believe what she had just witnessed. Eglit was 110 years old, but undoubtedly the coolest person she had ever met. And Vin wasn't too bad either.

Back at The Hangman's Noose, things had livened up. The cap'n had taken his seat and ordered the prisoners to stand in the corner nearest to him. He wanted to hear what they had to say. As for the rest of the gathering, he invited them to get a beer and either stand or take a seat.

'We must wait until they bring the littlun back. We don't want to keep a mother from her child, now do we, lads?'

There was laughter aplenty at the last comment, and the cap'n was enjoying the atmosphere. He turned and looked at the cowering prisoners and was noticeably angry that the Baldwins seemed unafraid, with Mrs Baldwin continuing to glare at him with eyes showing absolute defiance.

It was a good half an hour later when the door flew open and the others came in.

'Where's the girl?' asked the cap'n.

'We almost had 'er Cap'n, but there was magic Cap'n, voodoo.' The man trembled as he continued. 'The spirits have 'er now, Cap'n.'

The Baldwins just stood there. What did he mean, voodoo? More to the point, what spirits have got Lizzie? Whatever it was, something had definitely scared the men senseless.

'I must think what to do about the girl. Now to this lot. What have you got to say in your defence? Why did you come into our world?'

'You know why we're here,' piped up Charlie, 'you stole our chest.'

'We think of it as you finding our chest and us merely collecting it. Let me ask you a question, boy. If you lose a possession and someone else finds it, is it yours or theirs?'

'Well, it's mine, of course.'

'There we are, lads, guilty as charged.'

'What about the law of salvage?' yelled Mr Baldwin, trying to stop Charlie from getting into any more trouble.

'We're not at sea now. We're on an island in case you haven't noticed.'

'And why should it be your treasure and not ours?' said Mrs Baldwin with a steely determination.

'Because it's Calico Jack Rackham's treasure, that's him there,' he said, pointing to the painting above his right shoulder. 'And that's his wife, Anne Bonny,' pointing over his left shoulder. 'They had a son together, and that's where I come from.'

Mrs Baldwin hadn't noticed the portraits before, but as she looked, she had a strong sense that she had seen them somewhere before. Then it hit her like a lightning bolt. Everything was beginning to make sense.

'They had only one child?'

'When they hanged the crew in Jamaica, Anne was with child, so had a stay of execution. She remained in

228

prison until she gave birth and was never heard of again. As to her fate, or that of the child, nobody knows.'

'Until now,' continued Mrs Baldwin, thinking on her feet. 'What if Anne Bonny had a daughter and escaped from Jamaica back to England? She didn't want anything to happen to her daughter; she had seen enough bloodshed by now. So as soon as she hit dry land, she continued her journey all the way to North Wales. No-one would recognise her there. For the last part of her disappearing act, she changed her name from Bonny to Bonner.'

'A lovely story, but what's that got to do with us?'

'Surely her descendants would have as much right to the treasure as you.'

'Take 'em away. By the boy's own admission, they're guilty. We'll do the sentencing tomorrow.'

Just as they were being manhandled back through the door, Mrs Baldwin, realising this was potentially their last chance, gave a shout.

'I'm of Anne Bonny and Calico Jack.'

Everything stopped. Mr Baldwin and Charlie stood there in amazement. Surely she was joking. The Wolfe brothers, not as brave as they had once thought, fought back the tears.

'Her portrait,' she continued, 'the locket she's wearing.'

Everyone turned towards the cap'n, who himself was peering over his left shoulder.

'Now, look around my neck.'

229

The cap'n looked once more at the portrait, then again at Mrs Baldwin. He rose from his chair and walked over to her, now with a distinct look in his eye, one of bewilderment.

As he got to Mrs Baldwin, he reached down and held the locket in his hand, studying it closely. On the front, it had a very ornate italic engraving, "J&A". Then he flicked it open with his thumb to reveal the two miniature portraits and he stood there, momentarily speechless.

'And where did you say this came from?'

'We have handed it down the female side of my family for years. My mother gave it to me, but before her it was her grandmother's; Granny Bonner's.'

The room fell silent. The cap'n stood there, deep in thought. Then he spoke.

'Untie these three! Cousin, welcome to Purgatory,' and he embraced Mrs Baldwin. 'Take those two vultures back to their cage, and this time keep their hands tied!'

Edward (or was it Peregrine) Wolfe started sobbing, only to be told by his brother to "man up", although he too appeared close to tears.

Mrs Baldwin asked the cap'n if he would allow her husband and Charlie to find Lizzie. She wouldn't trust anyone else, so sending any of the crew would be pointless. For security, she would stay with him, just to make sure they all came back.

The cap'n agreed, pointing them to the exit.

'You two, show 'em where to go,' he said to the two men by the door.

Charlie and his father were quite pleased to leave and be able to gather their thoughts. They had just witnessed the craziest ten minutes of their lives, ten minutes in which the book-reading, cake-eating Mrs Baldwin had shown her true colours. And what colours they were. They both strutted along the road with an element of pride; imagine, a pirate in the family!

But they also had a rather pressing matter to deal with, which was to find Lizzie. Mr Baldwin didn't think for an instant that spirits had whisked away her, but he knew something was afoot and was keen to find out what. He just wanted Lizzie back, safe and sound.

The two men took them as far as the woods, but refused point blank to go any further.

'She was up there when the spirits took 'er,' said the taller of the two, pointing towards the top of the incline.

'Thank you both,' said Mr Baldwin. 'Don't worry, we can take it from here.'

With that, he and Charlie strode off into the woods.

'Don't forget the traps, Dad. They could be anywhere.'

Mr Baldwin was already being careful. Once bitten, twice shy, he thought. As for Charlie, he and Lizzie had navigated it successfully before, so he was sure he could do so again. Without the need to be silent, they both called out for Lizzie as they went. This time, they used their pocket torches, which allowed them to continue at speed. As they neared the brow of the hill,

Mr Baldwin spotted something suspicious on the ground.

'It looks like a used banger,' he said to Charlie.

There was a slight movement in front of them. Charlie shone his torch and he and his father nearly died of fright as they saw a black figure with the skeletal face, standing on a rock, not three yards away.

Chapter 27: Of Pirate Blood

Charlie and his father heard laughter, which they recognised immediately as Lizzie's.

'It's Eglit,' she said, as Charlie shone the torch on his sister. 'He terrified the life out of the pirates. You should have seen him, Dad.'

'It was simply a bit of showmanship on my part and a lot of imagination and ignorance on theirs.'

Vin helped his grandfather down from the rock and they all chuckled.

Mr Baldwin then told the incredible story of what had happened in the village, it culminating in the discovery that his wife was a direct descendant of the pirates, Calico Jack and Anne Bonny!

Mr Baldwin couldn't thank Eglit and Vin enough for being there in Lizzie's hour of need. They'd put themselves at considerable risk in doing so. He could see from their reaction that the entire episode had brought a lot of unexpected excitement to them both. They were glad to have helped and been part of the operation.

Everyone agreed it would be far safer for Vin and Eglit if they returned home, whilst Mr Baldwin, Charlie and Lizzie headed back to see what was going on in the village. They would be quite safe according to Mr Baldwin. He just wished he could say the same for the Wolfes. But they would try their best to ensure a favourable outcome.

Lizzie was rather apprehensive as she entered the village. The last time she'd seen the villagers, they'd been in hot pursuit. They made their way to The Hangman's Noose and walked through the door. To their amazement, there stood Mrs Baldwin, encircled by the inhabitants, telling stories and drinking beer!

'Mum,' shouted Lizzie.

Her head turned, and she barged her way through the crowd, a huge smile on her face. She grabbed Lizzie, and much to her embarrassment, lifted her clean off the floor before giving her a kiss on the cheek.

With the Baldwins all together, Burty approached and apologised most profusely about the entire chain of events. He explained that the villagers always had "one of their own" on the outside to monitor things, and currently, this was Burty himself. Once they had aroused his suspicions by telling him that Catweazle had been in their room, he went to investigate. He found the treasure by chance, but once he had, it was his duty to return it as the pirate's code said that "each man should have his share". If the Baldwins had kept it, they would be stealing from every single one of them, and that just couldn't be right.

'But it's been lost for centuries. If we hadn't found it, you'd be none the wiser as to its existence,' said Charlie, a hollow feeling in his stomach again.

'It belonged to our ancestors, so by rights it's ours.'

'It would appear that it's our family's ancestors too, so it's as much ours as yours.' Charlie looked around at his family for support. They were all aware of the

234

situation now that he had told Lizzie. The treasure would solve everything. Come on, someone say something, he prayed to himself.

'Shall we discuss it with the cap'n?' said Burty, remaining cool.

'I don't think that'll be necessary, Burty,' said Mrs Baldwin, who had been getting on like a house on fire with her long-lost cousin and wanted to keep it that way.

Charlie looked at his mother in astonishment.

'At least we still have the other treasure,' said Lizzie.

'And you shall keep that one,' said Burty, smiling from ear to ear.

Charlie stood there, speechless.

'Right Eleanor,' said the cap'n, addressing Mrs Baldwin by her Christian name. 'What shall we do with the prisoners? Would you like me to make 'em disappear? I'd put 'em to work, but they don't look like they'd be much good at anything.'

'I've got an idea, Henry. It needs some more thought, but I think it might work.'

'Alright m'dear, now let's enjoy the family reunion before we all head off to bed. We've got an early start tomorrow. We need to get you back.'

The cap'n led Mrs Baldwin away, before grabbing a chair and plonking it down next to his. As for Mr Baldwin and the children, surrounded by their new friends, they exchanged stories of piracy and the modern world.

After a rather uncomfortable night, sleeping on solid wooden beds with grass-filled mattresses, the Baldwins, accompanied by the cap'n and three of his men, made their way back to the road. It amazed them they hadn't come to further mishap as they had to make all manner of diversion to avoid one various trap or another. In fact, Mr and Mrs Baldwin now felt incredibly lucky that they ended up in the net rather than one of the more "interesting" traps. The cap'n took pride in telling them about his particular favourite, another pit, but one which was heaving with red ants, which gave a rather nasty bite.

'Not deadly,' he said, 'but things do get rather noisy!'

'What about the Wolfe brothers?' Mr Baldwin asked his wife.

'We're letting them stew for a while. That way, the plan will have a better chance of success.'

As they got to the sign, they all said their farewells, and the Baldwins continued back to Burty's. It was still very early in the morning and they were all looking forward to another delicious breakfast prepared by Sandra. They would need it. There was still a lot of sorting out to do.

After breakfast, they all packed for the beach and began the trek back to Gravedigger's Bay. First things first, though, they needed to stop off at Eglit's Emporium for a few supplies, and perhaps a quick catch up. As they entered, it was as if the previous evening had never happened. There was Vin up his stepladder, stacking shelves.

'Good morning, you beautiful people.'

'And a wonderful morning to you, Vin,' said Mrs Baldwin. 'We need a few bits and bobs for the beach. Is your grandfather out the back?'

'He's still asleep, I'm afraid, but I'm sure he'll be up and about later.'

'Ok, we'll pop round and see you both on the way back.' She grabbed some things to take with them, paid, and left with a cheery wave.

Today would involve the entire family working as a team. Mrs Baldwin had told the cap'n about the bags of treasure that they had taken from the chest and hidden. They agreed it was best if they retrieve the bags, knowing precisely where they were, and that they would meet again that evening to sort everything out, including what to do with the Wolfe brothers.

But first things first, and to their most arduous task, they had to get the bags from Catweazle's. Hopefully, it would be easier than hiding them there. Anyway, this time there would be all four of them, so it shouldn't be a problem. That was the theory anyway.

As they dropped their stuff on the beach, they looked around. It was exactly as it had been on their first morning, the waves gently breaking onto the creamy-white sand. Best of all, they had the entire beach to themselves.

'Come on then,' said Charlie, following a quick swim, 'let's get it done.'

En route, they agreed that as Lizzie and Charlie knew the exact location of the bags, if the coast was clear, they should retrieve them. To save time and lessen the danger, they would go in together. Their parents would split up and keep a lookout for the returning Catweazle. As soon as they finished, they would regroup and head back to the beach.

Spotting the hut, they stopped, looking and listening for any sight or sound of Catweazle. Confident of being alone, the children carried on towards the hut. Their parents split up, Mr Baldwin moving to the left, his wife to the right. As they neared the hut, Charlie and Lizzie yelled out simultaneously whilst doing a rather lively dance.

'Arghh, arghh, arghh,' came the muffled cries, then suddenly they stopped.

Catweazle had, it seemed, taken a few precautions since the last unwelcome visit. He had placed some very prickly leaves on the ground and then covered them with a smattering of sand to render them invisible. Simple but effective, thought the children as the pain slowly subsided.

Next, there was a stifled "ouch" from their mother's direction. They couldn't see what happened, but as they found out later, she had sprung a trap that whipped a thin branch into the back of her legs; painful but not life threatening.

Mr Baldwin was rather content, having spotted a net containing three coconuts suspended from a branch. He looked up at them, smiling. It would take a better man than Catweazle to catch him out. What he had failed to notice was that the ground was alive with small red ants, the very same type the cap'n had spoken of, and they had just spotted lunch. Catweazle was perhaps more intelligent than he had given him credit for!

Confident of being alone, the children worked fast, and it wasn't long before they were on their return journey to the beach, bags of gold in hand.

'What's happened to your feet and ankles?' Mrs Baldwin asked her husband when she noticed the bright red blotches.

He met her question with a rather embarrassed silence.

Now that they had the gold, there was no time for mucking about, so they grabbed their things from the beach and headed back to Burty's. On their way, they made a minor detour to see if Blue was making any progress. It was a strange feeling. Before, they had wanted him to be making as much progress as possible, now they wanted him to be making none whatsoever.

'I have nothing more to report. You haven't seen the Wolfes by any chance? I was looking for them last night, but they weren't at the hotel.'

'If we see them, we'll tell them you'd like a word,' replied Mr Baldwin.

'Thanks. Oh, by the way, we're making progress on the skeletons. It needs final confirmation, but the team thinks they are the shipwrecked pirates from the story. It all seems to tie in. Very exciting news for the island.'

'That's fantastic. Let's hope it brings the island more business.'

'We need to be going,' said Mrs Baldwin. 'Thanks again, Blue.'

They nipped back to Burty's, refilling their bottles with water before setting off toward Purgatory. This time, they weren't letting the gold out of their sight until it was safely back in the chest.

Once past the sign, they busied themselves with retrieving the final two bags before carrying on up the hill and then back down to the village. They took great care in the route they took, scanning for anything that might look out of place.

Back in the village, they headed straight to The Hangman's Noose in search of the cap'n. Sure enough, there he sat, waiting for their return. They grabbed the bags of coins from their rucksacks and sidled over to the chest. Lifting the lid, they poured the contents in. They looked at the treasure again in wonder, as if seeing it for the first time. It was a truly magnificent sight.

'We still need to decide what to do with the prisoners, Eleanor, m'dear?'

'Well, I was thinking, Henry, they might not live here on the island, but we know where they live. Why not scare the living daylights out of them? It shouldn't be hard. They don't look like very brave men from what I've seen so far. Then you tell them that if they ever mention a word about any of this, there will be the most terrible repercussions.'

'I must see how they react, but I'll give it a try m'dear, just for you. You children, take your father and make yourselves scarce. Come on m'dear, you must practice something first if we want it to have the desired effect,' and with that the cap'n and his long-lost relative left whilst his men went and fetched the prisoners, with a very specific set of instructions.

Inside the Hangman's Noose, all was calm, so the noise of the crowd outside caught everyone's attention. All eyes were on the door as it opened and the brothers, hands tightly bound in front of them, fell to the floor. They were a sorry sight, slumped, sobbing, every bit of resistance long since gone. Two burly men came forward, lifting them each in turn, looping their hands over hooks high overhead, so they now resembled something from a butcher's shop window. Although tall, even at full stretch, they could only just touch the floor. As the time ticked by, so their nerves deteriorated further, something the cap'n and Mrs Baldwin had banked on. They needed everything to be perfect. This had to be a performance the brothers would never forget.

The door suddenly flew open and there stood the cap'n, in full uniform, complete with tricorn hat and cutlass. He cut a dashing figure, striding in, all eyes upon him, before turning and gesturing back to the doorway. There stood Mrs Baldwin, hair tied back beneath her hat, wearing a white ruffle shirt and some dark brown breeches. On her hip lay a cutlass, with an enormous ruby inset on the handle.

'I believe you know mi cousin,' said the cap'n.

'Yes, yes, we do.'

241

'And are you afeard of me?' he said, glaring at them with eyes like daggers, his men cheering and jeering in the background.

'Yes,' came the timid reply.

'What did ye say?' he bellowed back, eyes wide.

'Yes, Cap'n.'

'Well, if ye's afeard of me then by heavens ye should be afeard of mi cousin, I've just seen what she's capable of!'

The brothers looked at each other, terrified. What manner of horror had the cap'n just witnessed.

Chapter 28: The Dancing Chicken

Mrs Baldwin strode over to the prisoners. She took her cutlass from her belt and, whilst staring at them coldly and unblinkingly, drew the point of the cutlass under each of their chins. As tears gathered in their eyes, she leapt, turning a full three hundred and sixty degrees and brought the blade flashing above their heads, cutting through the rope holding them to the beams. The Wolfe brothers slumped to the floor.

'Feed them to the sharks,' she said.

'Wait m'dear,' said the cap'n. 'You know where they live, don't you?'

'Yes Henry, why do you ask?'

'What if they promised, on their honour, never to breathe a word about what they have seen or heard on the island?'

'We won't say a word, we promise. Please. Believe us. We won't say a word.'

'I'll leave the decision to you, Henry, but I think we're safer if we use them as shark bait.'

'How do I know you'll honour your word?'

'She knows where we live, Cap'n, she knows where we live!' they sobbed.

That was good enough for the cap'n.

'Right, I'll take you at your word. But if I ever hear it's been broken, there will be consequences, wherever you may be. Take 'em to the sign lads and send 'em on their way.'

Outside the window, Mr Baldwin looked at his children. None of them could believe what they had just witnessed. He and Charlie looked at each other wide-eyed. Lizzie just crouched there, beaming with pride.

With the Wolfe brothers well out of sight, Mr Baldwin and the children went back into The Hangman's Noose. Mrs Baldwin and the cap'n were sitting on their chairs, laughing hysterically.

'The bit about feeding 'em to the sharks was brilliant m'dear,' said the cap'n.

'I was quite proud of that. Did I get close to their hands when I cut them down? I didn't really notice.' This sent them both into fits of laughter once again.

'Get everyone in lads, it's time for distributing the treasure.'

In seconds, the place was heaving, and the cap'n walked over to the chest.

'Right mi'hearties, the Master has counted everything and with everyone taking one share, the Master one share and a quarter and Eleanor and I one share and a half, there'll be two coins left. I reckon we should give 'em to the two young'uns who found the treasure. After all, they are of pirate blood. All in favour say "aye".'

'Aye,' came the resounding cheer.

Every person in the room stepped forward and collected four coins from the Master, who kept five for himself and gave the cap'n and Mrs Baldwin six each. Finally, he gave the two beaming children one doubloon each.

244

'Sorry Dad,' said Lizzie smiling, 'you're not of pirate blood.'

The party was in full swing when Mr Baldwin suggested they leave. It was getting late and they should get back and have dinner. With a lot of fond farewells, they left the village, but not before Mrs Baldwin had done a quick change back to her normal attire. The cap'n was quite insistent that she kept the clothes and, in particular, the cutlass. After all, he said, it was Anne Bonny's. With a rather large bag under her arm and family in tow, Eleanor Baldwin made her way along the track to the road, and in no time at all, they were opening up the doors to their rooms.

'What day is it?' asked Mr Baldwin in a mild panic.

'Friday, why?' answered Charlie.

'My goodness, we're going home tomorrow, and we haven't even said goodbye to Vin and Eglit; or Blue. Let's have an early dinner and get everything packed this evening. We'll get up early and say all our goodbyes first thing.'

The next morning came all too soon for the children. They had already packed their bags and so lay on their beds talking about the holiday of a lifetime they had just had. They had entered a different world for a while, kept secret from the rest of civilisation for centuries. The most exciting thing of all; somehow they were part of that world.

Mrs Baldwin knocked on the adjoining door.

'Are you children ready for breakfast?'

'Just coming.'

Over breakfast, they talked about the morning's farewells. They would start with Blue and see if he had any more updates, and finish with Vin and Eglit. One thing that Mrs Baldwin had remembered was the extra coin that Blue had given back to Lizzie. She felt very guilty, as it meant that they now had an extra coin, and somehow that just wasn't right. But she had an idea, as long as the children were game.

'Lizzie, I believe you still have the coin Blue gave back to you.'

'Crikey, I'd forgotten about that.'

'I think we all had. Can you two take it to Catweazle's shack straight after breakfast and leave it on the table for him? After all, without him we would never have found the treasure again; or Purgatory.'

The children's faces lit up. Unexpectedly, one last adventure was beckoning!

Annoyingly, it turned out to be a rather boring affair. They knew all about his traps and with no sign of Catweazle, they waltzed straight into the hut without a care in the world. As Lizzie reached into her pocket for the coin, there was a shriek as Catweazle pounced on them from his hiding place amongst the beams.

'Stop,' pleaded Charlie, 'stop! We have something for you.'

Catweazle looked up, and Lizzie held out her hand.

'We thought you might like this.'

A tear formed in Catweazle's eye. 'Thank you.'

'The pirates have the rest, but it is theirs, so perhaps that's best.'

Catweazle got up, staring at the coin, and started dancing, arms and legs everywhere. It appeared his lifelong quest was over.

'But you must swear never to tell anyone where it came from,' said Charlie. 'This is our secret.'

Catweazle looked at him and nodded, then resumed his celebrations, which were still going on as the children quietly left.

When they got back to Burty's, they found their parents having a coffee and talking to Sandra.

'Right children, let's make a move,' said Mr Baldwin.

They finished their coffees, stood up, and headed to the door.

'You never brought me those lobsters,' said Sandra.

'We were just too busy, I'm afraid,' said Charlie.

'Next time,' she said, smiling.

Two minutes later, they found themselves outside Blue's. He opened the door, and it was clear from the smile on his face he was exceptionally happy.

'Good morning, Blue, how are you?' said Mr Baldwin.

'Great thanks, we've had some mighty fine news.'

The Baldwin family went momentarily rather quiet.

'The skeletons, he said, they are three hundred years old, so they were the pirates. Imagine, pirates on this island. It will be fantastic for visitors and locals alike. More visitors, more trade. And it's all down to you!'

Their eyes lit up as they realised just how much it would mean to the island.

'Any other news?' asked Mrs Baldwin, hoping there wasn't. 'It's just that we're off in a couple of hours.'

'Nothing at all, I'm afraid. To be honest, I think the chest and its contents are long gone.'

'If you ever need us, Burty has our contact details in the UK. Anyway, it's been great to meet you. Take care and see you again one day hopefully,' said Mr Baldwin.

'You have a safe trip home and thanks again. We'll miss you.'

They turned and headed towards Eglit's Emporium.

'Morning Vin,' said Charlie as they entered the store, 'is your grandfather out the back?'

'Good morning all. I'm afraid he's in bed. I think he's still recovering from the other night's exertions. We thought you were coming around yesterday afternoon.'

'Apologies for that,' said Mrs Baldwin. 'We had some things to sort out, as you can imagine. They took a little longer than we thought. We came to say goodbye. We're off shortly.'

'He'll be sorry to have missed you. I know he wanted to show the children one of his other outfits, his witch doctor's one. It's covered in feathers and looks magnificent.'

'Thank you, Vin,' said Lizzie as she ran up and hugged him. She would never forget what he and Eglit had done for her in her hour of need.

'It was our pleasure, young lady. We haven't had fun like that in years. Oh, and you might want this.'

He reached across and grabbed a copy of The Gazette from the newspaper rack.

The children beamed as they saw their photograph on the front page with the headline "Skeletons Discovered in Whaler's Bay".

'Thank you, Vin,' said Charlie and Lizzie in unison.

'Give our best to your grandfather. We'll never forget him,' said Mrs Baldwin. 'And thanks to you too.'

Vin gave them a hug each before they turned and continued on their way.

Back at Betty's Guesthouse, they grabbed the bags from their rooms and made their way to Reception to check out. Sandra said she was sorry to see them go and gave them a bag full of goodies for the journey. Mrs Baldwin immediately popped it all into her bag "for safety". Burty came out of the office when he heard their voices to say his farewells. They had organised a taxi earlier, and as they were talking, they heard Tallboy pull up outside.

'If you ever want a room on the island, just call. I will always have one available,' Burty said, looking in Mrs Baldwin's direction.

'Thanks,' said Charlie, 'I'm sure Lizzie and I will be back, with or without our parents!'

With one last goodbye, they grabbed their bags and headed to the car.

'Good morning you beautiful people, I hope you all had a nice relaxing holiday. Not much goes on here.

249

That's what makes it such a great place to come and unwind.'

'We found the skeletons,' Lizzie reminded him.

'You did; that's our excitement done for the next twenty years,' he said.

Tallboy put their bags in the boot, and everyone climbed in. They had once again forgotten how much of a squeeze it was with Tallboy in the car with them.

They had left plenty of time to get to the airport as they had anticipated driving the entire way there at walking pace. And sure enough, that is exactly what happened, with Tallboy not even getting out of his preferred second gear. No-one complained though, this was probably the most relaxing part of the entire holiday!

As they pulled up, they could see their plane waiting for them on the tarmac. It was a sad moment. Departing the island was proving more difficult than they thought. It wasn't as if they had made a few acquaintances; they were leaving behind some real friends.

'Don't worry, I'm sure we'll be back. After all, we still have to return the pole and the rope to Sharky,' said Mr Baldwin, winking at the children.

Then he got out his wallet and paid Tallboy, leaving him a big tip.

'Thanks Tallboy, it's been a pleasure.'

'The pleasure has been all mine. See you again soon, I hope.'

As the Baldwins sat with their bags in the departure lounge, Charlie finally plucked up the courage to speak to his father.

'Dad,' there was hesitation in his voice. 'As we only kept some of the gold, will we still have to move?' The butterflies in his stomach were working overtime. He needed to hear the answer, as terrifying as it might be.

'Sorry, Charlie, I don't understand.'

'Before we left, I heard you and Mum talking about having to move to a smaller house because you've lost your job.' He couldn't hide his sadness and was feeling sick.

'Not at all. They offered me the chance to move to the other office. I thought a slice of big city life might be a bit of an adventure, but I think we've had enough excitement for the time being. What do you think?' He looked across at his wife, who was positively beaming.

Charlie looked at his mother and then across to his sister. Nobody, not even their father, could contain their smile.

'Thanks, Dad. And if you ever get bored again, let me and Lizzie know and we'll hunt for another map.'

A young man came in to pick up their bags and asked them to follow him to the plane. They were the only passengers booked on the flight, so as soon as they had loaded their luggage and buckled their seat belts, the door closed and the engines sparked into life. As they taxied to the end of the runway, the children looked at each other with great sadness. They knew

251

they would probably never have a holiday like this one again.

Hysterical laughter suddenly interrupted the sound of the engines. Once the captain had gathered himself slightly, he made an announcement.

'The flight might be delayed for a minute or two as there seems to be an enormous half-plucked chicken by the edge of the runway.'

The entire family stared out of the small circular windows. By the road, they noticed Vin waving. Beside him there was a shopping trolley full of cushions. The children smiled, and as the engines roared into life ready for take-off, they spotted something coming into view. As they stared out of the window, they saw a man, five feet tall, wearing nothing but a grass skirt, a small cape and headdress, all adorned with brightly coloured feathers. His arms and legs were weathered and rather scrawny, but so they should be for someone 110 years old. And he wasn't just waving, he seemed to be doing a rather strange dance, almost as if he had ants in his pants.

He watched their faces at the windows as they swept past and gave a gigantic smile and waved. This had been one of the best weeks of his life, too!

Printed in Great Britain
by Amazon